# All Our Worldly Goods

BY THE SAME AUTHOR (IN ENGLISH)

*Suite Française*
*David Golder*
*Le Bal* (including *Snow in Autumn*)
*Fire in the Blood*
*The Courilof Affair*

## TRANSLATOR'S NOTE

Irène Némirovsky's *All Our Worldly Goods* first appeared in French as *Les Biens de ce monde*, in 1947, five years after the author's murder at Auschwitz. The novel opens just before the outbreak of World War I and ends just after the start of World War II. Like *Suite Française*, it tells the stories of families whose lives intertwine, and does so with the astute psychological and social observation for which Némirovsky is now known. Unlike *Suite Française*, the novel is complete, and it is clear that Némirovsky was not writing under the ominous premonition of her impending death. In this work, there is an underlying feeling of hope that makes *Suite Française* all the more heartrending. In fact, together the two books provide a panoramic view of life in France from 1911 to 1940.

*All Our Worldly Goods* is about love: forbidden love, married love, unrequited love, the love of parents for their children, of people for their homes, of citizens for their country. The title in French – almost impossible to translate with all its nuances – manages to encapsulate both the spiritual and material aspects of '*les biens*', the good things of this life, in every sense of the term. We have chosen *All Our Worldly Goods* because it evokes something of the French in both senses, as well as recalling traditional marriage vows. With the skill and subtlety so characteristic of her writing, Némirovsky offers us entry into the lives of people who belong to another world, one long gone, but whose emotions – desires, fears, suffering, pride, happiness and determination to live fulfilled lives – remain universal.

Translating Irène Némirovsky is always a joy but I also owe a great deal to my editor, Rebecca Carter, whose insights, professionalism, encouragement and friendship have been invaluable.

Sandra Smith
Robinson College
Cambridge, June 2008

# IRÈNE NÉMIROVSKY

# All Our Worldly Goods

*Translated from the French by Sandra Smith*

Chatto & Windus
LONDON

Published by Chatto & Windus 2008

2 4 6 8 10 9 7 5 3 1

First published in France as *Les Biens de ce monde* by Éditions Albin Michel 1947

First published in Great Britain in 2008 by
Chatto & Windus
Random House, 20 Vauxhall Bridge Road,
London SW1V 2SA
www.rbooks.co.uk

Addresses for companies within The Random House Group Limited can be found at:
www.randomhouse.co.uk/offices.htm

The Random House Group Limited Reg. No. 954009

A CIP catalogue record for this book
is available from the British Library

Hardback ISBN 9780701182137
Trade Paperback ISBN 9780701182144

The Random House Group Limited supports The Forest Stewardship
Council (FSC), the leading international forest certification organisation.
All our titles that are printed on Greenpeace approved FSC certified paper carry the
FSC logo. Our paper procurement policy can be found at
www.rbooks.co.uk/environment

**Mixed Sources**
Product group from well-managed
forests and other controlled sources
www.fsc.org  Cert no. TT-COC-2139
© 1996 Forest Stewardship Council

Typeset by Palimpsest Book Production Limited, Grangemouth, Stirlingshire

Printed and bound in Great Britain by CPI Mackays Ltd, Chatham ME5 8TD

# 1

They were together, so they were happy. Even though the watchful family slipped between them, separating them gently but firmly, the young man and woman knew they were near one another; nothing else mattered. It was the beginning of the century – an autumn evening at the seaside, overlooking the English Channel. Pierre and Agnès, their parents and Pierre's fiancée had all gathered to watch the last firework display of summer. On the fine sand of the dunes, the inhabitants of Wimereux-Plage formed dark little groups, barely visible in the starlight. The moist sea air drifted around them. A profound sense of tranquillity reigned over them, and over the sea, and over the world.

The families were not very friendly to each other, for they belonged to different social classes: the bourgeoisie didn't mingle with the lower middle classes. Each kept its place and its distance with modesty, steadfastness and dignity. Each built itself a fortress out of spades and folding chairs. Each scrupulously respected the possessions of its neighbours and defended its own courteously but resolutely, just as a well-tempered sword bends but does not break. The mothers would murmur, 'Don't touch that, it doesn't belong to you . . . Excuse me Madame, this is my son's seat and this one is mine . . . Watch your toys or someone will take them.'

Heavy storm clouds had been gathering all day, but it hadn't rained. Agnès thought how wonderful it would be to dip her bare feet in the water. But it wasn't done to go into the sea, except at midday and amid a crowd of people, thus somehow preserving a young girl's modesty. She could hear Pierre sighing. He didn't like the heat. He was wearing a dark jacket with a stiff collar; its pale white glow allowed her to make him out in the darkness. He was lying in the hollow of a sand dune, impatiently waving his arms. 'Pierre, come now, sit still,' his mother said, as if he were twelve years old. In fact he was twenty-four, but her tender, authoritarian voice held such power over him that he obeyed her still. Simone, Pierre's fiancée, sat between him and Agnès; he turned away to avoid looking at the pale folds of flesh round Simone's waist and her milky-white round arms. This girl looks as if she's made of milk, and butter, and cream, he mused. It was strange; he had often looked with pleasure at her fresh, plump body, her thick, soft waist and red hair. But, for some time now, the sight of her made him feel nauseous, like a meal that is too heavy, too sweet. Nevertheless, they were engaged. The following week, a grand engagement dinner would make it official, uniting the two families. There was no hope for him and Agnès. So little hope that they hadn't even confessed their love to each other. It was pointless. Pierre Hardelot came from the Hardelot Paper Mills family of Saint-Elme. Agnès's family were brewers. Only a foreigner, someone from outside, would have thought a marriage between them possible. The people of Saint-Elme had no such illusions; *they* understood, with infallible, subtle tact, how the two young people's different social standing was a barrier. The brewers were from the lower classes and, even worse, they weren't from the region but from Flanders. The Hardelots were from Saint-Elme. There were plenty more obstacles. Pierre should have felt despair, but in spite of everything he was happy. Agnès was here. They were together.

The fireworks still hadn't started. The men allowed themselves to relax a little; they stretched out their legs, propped themselves up on their elbows. 'No one else is lolling about like you,' Pierre's mother whispered in his ear. 'It isn't done.' The women sat on the beach as if they were in drawing-room armchairs, backs straight, skirts modestly covering their ankles. If a blade of pale dune grass bent in the wind to tickle their calves, they closed their legs tight, as if ashamed. Their dresses were long and black; their starched linen collars, stiffened with whalebone, restricted their necks, forcing them to turn their heads from side to side with sudden, staccato movements, like hens pecking at worms. When the lighthouse beacon passed you could see their hats, a veritable garden of chiffon and velvet flowers quivering on wire stems. Here and there a stuffed seagull with a pointy beak stood perched on a straw boater. This was the height of fashion, the favourite adornment of the season, though some people found it somewhat daring. There was something unsubtle about that bird, with its little glass eye and extended wings, Pierre's mother thought, as she looked at Agnès's mother, comparing her neighbour's grey-feathered hat to her own with its decoration of daisies. But Agnès's mother was from Paris. There were niceties she couldn't sense, couldn't understand.

Nevertheless, she seemed very anxious to please. 'Yes,' she would say, 'I do agree', or 'That's what I think as well'. But even her humility did not inspire confidence. Everyone knew that, before her marriage, Gabrielle Florent had been forced to work for a living. She herself admitted that she'd given singing lessons. Anything was possible. A singing teacher might have socialised with actresses. In spite of everything, she was accepted in Saint-Elme, for, as far as her present conduct was concerned, there was nothing to be said. Yet even though she was accepted, people remained on the defensive.

It would have been better for Agnès, for Agnès's future, if there had been some precise accusation regarding her mother's past, rather than these vague insinuations, people whispering, nodding or sighing as she passed by. 'Do they have family in Paris? I think this Madame Florent had a bad reputation when she was young. Her daughter will not find a husband so easily. I can't see her getting married. Can you?' Monsieur Florent had died three years before. Everyone was surprised that his widow had remained in Saint-Elme. 'She must have no family left,' people said, slightly maliciously; in the eyes of Saint-Elme, the absence of numerous relatives was suspicious. 'She says she's lost everyone.' That was no excuse. A good middle-class family should be large, and hardy enough to stand up to death.

'The fireworks,' shouted the children, 'the fireworks are starting.'

A golden swirl burst forth from behind the sand dunes and spun over the waves. Everyone stood up in curiosity and pleasure. The inhabitants of Wimereux-Plage rarely indulged in entertainments; they played Ludo in the Casino and, sometimes, touring theatre companies came from Paris. They didn't have to pay to see the fireworks. Sound economic principles reigned supreme here.

'Come over here, Agnès,' said Pierre. 'Come and stand in front of me, so you can see better . . .'

But when Agnès went over to him, she found him flanked by his mother and fiancée. He held out his hand to help her climb on to the sand dune and Madame Hardelot immediately called out to her husband, 'Charles, stand behind Agnès. You're so tall! She can't see a thing, can you, darling?'

And so, protected on three sides, Pierre was as defended as a fortress. He pushed the women away rather briskly. 'It's too hot. I prefer lying in the sand.'

Agnès didn't dare move. She lowered her head and choked back the tears.

During the winter the Hardelots and Florents rarely saw each other, even though they were neighbours. The people of Saint-

Elme had a remarkable talent for ignoring whatever they didn't wish to know. How well they knew when to become deaf and blind. How tactfully they side-stepped anything they found unpleasant! Families could live next door to one another for twenty years and never even glance at each other. But here, at Wimereux, it was different. In their youth, Agnès's father and Charles Hardelot had each bought property on the seafront; their chalets were adjoining. It was unfortunate, but as this was a good location, it took precedence over any other factor. They couldn't very well ignore each other. And besides, summer was of no consequence, the Hardelots thought; it was as if their habits, their prejudices, their preconceptions were all part of their environment, their habitat. Once away from home, they became more tolerant, just as certain insects lose their sting once outside the hive. But summer was nearly over. 'And we'll never see each other again,' thought Agnès. 'He'll get married and as for me . . . Anyway, does he even love me? He's never told me he does . . . He knows he can't marry me, so it wouldn't be right,' she thought. 'But if he did love me, I'd follow him to the ends of the earth.'

'Look how beautiful it is,' said Madame Florent, leaning towards her daughter.

'Oh, yes, beautiful,' replied Agnès, her voice trembling, seeing nothing.

A spray of shooting stars rose towards the sky, then fell back down again, lighting up the crowd; a long whistle sounded as it descended, like a jet of steam. Everyone looked up: Pierre, thin and suntanned, with his wide forehead, small mouth and light-brown moustache; Madame Hardelot, fat, soft and pale; Simone, with her heavy chin. Agnès automatically imitated the movements of the others; she had a young, thin face, pale skin and dark hair.

Flames, cornucopias, fiery wheels filled the skies. Then they went out. The night seemed even darker; the air smelled of smoke. Only one little green shooting star, as lost as an orphan, hovered for a moment in the sky before plunging at great speed towards the sand dunes. 'Oh!' the crowd sighed in disappointment, but then other fireworks lit up the east (a cockerel, a fountain, white at first, then tinged with silver, then with red, white and blue) and the crowd showed its joy by crying out a satisfied 'Ah-ah-ah . . .' while the wails of a child rose from the darkness.

The fountain exploded and fell silent. The last rockets disappeared into the sea. The fireworks were over. The Florents and the Hardelots set off for home. Charles Hardelot led the way. His spectacles, set low on his nose, glistened in the beam from the lighthouse. He held his shoes and socks in his hands; he had rolled his trouser legs above his knees. It was difficult to walk in the dunes unless you were barefoot; the hills and valleys of sand were constantly shifting, then re-forming, setting off fine white rivers that crunched inside stockings and ankle boots. It was a constant trial to these ladies; they walked with difficulty, grimacing, leaning against each other. Naturally, the idea of taking off their shoes would never have occurred to them, any more than the idea of removing their corsets. The young women walked alongside their mothers, in silence. Pierre was gone.

'He said he was going over to the Casino before coming home,' said Madame Hardelot disapprovingly. Then she whispered in her husband's ear, 'Don't go to bed before he gets back so you know what time he comes in . . .'

'Do you want to know what I think?' said Charles, in the same tone of voice. 'I'll feel better when we're back in Saint-Elme and Pierre is married. I dislike these excessive seaside distractions,' he added, rubbing his thin dry legs; the sand fell from his tight, muscular calves and long, delicate ankles. He put his shoes back on, shaking his head with a worried expression.

A few street lamps were lit along the road, illuminating the houses set among the sand dunes and pine trees. They had names like 'My Respite', 'My Delight', 'The Swiss Chalet' or 'The

Waves'. They were all alike, with their high pointed roofs and wooden balconies, their narrow windows decorated with pebbles and seashells. The Hardelots and the Florents had the last two houses. Beyond them, the road turned into a sandy slope. Sand covered the front steps and the garden paths.

Wimereux was already getting ready for a peaceful night. Here and there, a light flickered behind the shutters, then went out. Each household barricaded itself in to keep out the nocturnal wind, the roaring sea. There was no singing; no shouting: the people of Wimereux were 'respectable'. Further down the coast, a luxury hotel had been built, so they'd heard; its guests were gentlemen who dressed for dinner every evening, and ladies who went riding every day. Down there, they danced and gambled until dawn. But no one envied those outsiders. That sort of thing went on far away, or so it seemed, on another planet, one that deserved neither interest nor consideration of any sort. As they went inside, the families exchanged long, ceremonious goodbyes. Sleepy children were dragged along by the hand. In single file, they climbed the pale wooden steps that smelled of sap and honey. Simone went into her room; it was between Pierre's grandfather's room and his parents' bedroom. Pierre slept on a different floor, as far away from his fiancée as possible, so as not to arouse the slightest suspicion about the fact that a young man and young woman were living under the same roof. Doors were bolted; windows locked; they checked under the beds. In their peaceful universe, these people saw danger everywhere, pitfalls of every kind.

In her room, Agnès lifted a corner of the curtain, looking down the road for Pierre. She was very careful not to be seen. What a scandal it would be if anyone suspected she wasn't asleep, that she was waiting . . . for whom? Someone else's fiancé. He wasn't there. A soft but thick fog rose from the sea. It was early September; you could smell autumn now. The air had lost its warmth, become damp and bitter. She waited. It was nearly midnight. One by one, the street lamps went out. At midnight, all of Wimereux was asleep. Finally, finally, she heard the long creak of the little wooden door, pushed open by Pierre. He was home. He wasn't coming home to her, but to Simone; yet in spite of everything he was home. She stood beside the window for a moment longer, gently removing the pins that held up her long hair. The beach, the sea, were invisible, covered in mist. All that could be heard was a very faint murmur wafting up from the waves, like the sound of someone sighing.

2

Madame Florent and Madame Hardelot were going for a swim.
They had shared the hire of a beach hut. A horse pulled a faded
little caravan towards the sea; inside it, the ladies were undressing.
Out of modesty, they each kept to one side of a makeshift curtain
made of towels. The horse plodded slowly along; sun filled the
beach hut. They had gone past the sand dunes, the thistles, the
place where wild little pink carnations grew. They were nearly at
the water's edge. Through the small window, Madame Hardelot
waved at her husband who was fishing for prawns; at his waist
hung a little wicker basket with the words 'Wimereux-Plage'
embroidered in red; his old felt hat was dripping wet; in one hand
he held his net, in the other his spectacles which kept falling off.
Charles's innocent enjoyment of simple pleasures caused his wife
regret that the summer holidays were coming to an end. Otherwise,
she was happy to be going home to Saint-Elme and her routine.
Standing there in her pink corset, large, flabby and pale, vague
thoughts passed through her mind: that the water would be cold,
that Madame Florent would make little shrieking noises when
diving in. She thought about Pierre, about the engagement dinner,
about that girl Agnès, so obviously in love with Pierre, about the

engagement ring (how expensive everything was!), about Simone's dowry, about love, marriage, life. Taking off her black cotton stockings and rolling them up, she let out soft sighs.

As Madame Florent got undressed, she glanced every so often at the mirror hanging on the wall; she had managed to arrange for the only mirror available to be on her side of the beach hut. She was feeling rather melancholy. The forthcoming marriage between Pierre and Simone aroused strong emotions in both mothers: one of them felt the sweet satisfaction of having the rich dowry of an orphaned child come into the family; the other felt frustrated. Not that she held out any hope for Agnès. The Hardelots had made it abundantly clear that they considered such a marriage undesirable. But it was upsetting to see other people getting married and not Agnès, upsetting and unfair. Obviously, her mother thought, she couldn't compete with Simone when it came to money, but there was no comparison as far as her good looks, her figure, her hair were concerned – *my* good looks, *my* figure, *my* hair, when I was young. Those things count, after all. She looks like a cow, that Simone. And then, following this train of thought, she said out loud, 'Your future daughter-in-law really has a delightful nature. So calm . . . docile even. What a valuable quality in a wife! I do admire it. I'm exactly the opposite. I live off my nerves. And her lovely skin and beautiful hair!'

'Yes, she's a good girl,' said Madame Hardelot, instinctively adopting the modest, satisfied tone of someone with the upper hand. Nevertheless, she couldn't praise Simone without having some reservations: it wasn't proper to appear overly happy about having arranged this marriage. Simone would do, of course, but wasn't her son better?

'I find her rather shy,' Madame Hardelot continued after a moment's silence, 'and her personality isn't perhaps exactly as you think . . .'

She lowered her voice, even though she could only be overheard by the sky, the air and the waves. 'She likes to seem easy-going. She's not always so willing.'

'She's never had the calming influence of a mother,' said Madame Florent sympathetically. 'She lost hers when she was very young, didn't she?'

'Yes, very young,' Madame Hardelot said quickly, wishing, as they say in the theatre, not to miss a cue, sensing some disagreeable remark in the air.

But Madame Florent insisted on taking advantage of the opportunity. 'Yes, it's odd that she died so young . . .' she said. 'And yet, Simone seems to be in excellent health, doesn't she?'

'Her mother died of a broken heart, after she was widowed,' Madame Hardelot said curtly, adding triumphantly, 'As for her father, he died in a car accident.'

Madame Florent fell silent. And anyway, Simone looked so robust that it wasn't really possible to insinuate anything about her physical condition.

So all she said was, 'Simone bears a remarkable resemblance to one of my friends, who married young. The poor girl . . . she never had any children. That sometimes happens, you know, with these chubby, rosy-cheeked women.'

'Shall we stop the horse?' asked Madame Hardelot, looking anxiously at the rising waves; they were as high as the running board of the caravan. 'Are you ready?'

'Yes, just coming.'

They stepped outside, both wearing black wool swimming suits consisting of a tunic pulled in tightly at the waist with wide, billowing pantaloons. The wind coming in from the sea made their tunics flutter in every direction and got under their canvas swimming hats, making them swell up like balloons. Madame Hardelot's was bright green; Madame Florent's was orange.

Just as they were about to get into the water, the ladies hesitated;

Madame Florent dipped her little toe in. 'It's so cold!' she exclaimed.

They stood at the doorway of the hut; every now and then they leaned forward to test the water; they both wore gold wedding bands.

'You'll have so much to do, so much to think about this winter, my dear Madame Hardelot ... with a wedding to organise at home. But such joy as well!'

Madame Hardelot shaded her eyes from the sun and smiled. The obvious displeasure of Madame Florent allowed her to feel her own happiness. And so, sitting comfortably, without her corset, her arms and legs bare and relaxed, out in the fresh air, in the sunshine, she felt extremely peaceful; she felt happy, as if she had everything she could wish for. She had a husband she loved, the best son in the world. The paper factory was flourishing. Her mother-in-law was dead. Pierre was making an excellent marriage. She thanked divine Providence with all her heart for having scattered roses on her path while giving her the fortitude to bear their thorns in a Christian way: her father-in-law's nature, the bad conduct of Josephine, the new maid. She was feeling charitable.

She looked at Madame Florent with indulgence. The poor woman, widowed, alone in the world ... 'But what are you waiting for?' she asked.

'What do you mean?'

'Well ... shouldn't it be Agnès's turn to get married soon?'

The two women looked at each other. Madame Florent's eyes said, 'Are you just saying that? ... Or do you have someone in mind?' and Madame Hardelot's smile replied, 'Why not make someone else happy as long as my own happiness is not at stake?'

She nodded kindly several times. 'I've been thinking ...'

At that very moment a wave, more powerful than the others,

broke at the foot of the caravan, crashing loudly over the running board. With cries and laughter, the two women hopped about and then, finally, clambered down into the water.

'Oh my goodness! It's so cold. My back's all wet.'

'Jump in. Just jump right in!'

'You first.'

'No, you first – show me how it's done.'

Even though they were enjoying themselves, they didn't lose their train of thought.

'Who does she have in mind?' Madame Florent wondered, splashing water on to her back and shivering with both fear and pleasure at the feel of the fresh, cold sea. 'Who could it be?' She knew all the eligible young men in Saint-Elme.

Meanwhile, Madame Hardelot gently bobbed up and down with the waves; she flailed her arms about and imagined she was swimming. The current brought the women together, then pushed them apart again.

'Is it someone I know?' Madame Florent finally shouted out, her patience wearing thin.

Madame Hardelot nodded yes, smiling.

'A decent man?'

'Of course, my dear, would I even suggest him otherwise?' replied Madame Hardelot, pausing a moment to spit out a mouthful of salty water.

'Is he the right age; does he have a good job and some money?'

'There's a slight difference in age.'

'Really?'

'He's about forty . . .'

'I don't know if Agnès . . .'

'It's up to you to make her see reason. He's Lumbres's son.'

'Lumbres?' said Madame Florent, disappointed, 'but they're shopkeepers.'

The Lumbres were watchmakers in Saint-Omer.

'Shopkeepers who bled themselves dry to educate their son. He's a doctor now with a good position.'

She waited for a moment and then called out over the crest of a wave, 'In Paris . . .'

'Oh, so now we've come to the bottom of it,' thought Madame Florent, smiling to herself. 'Agnès, married and living in Paris, far away from the newlyweds. That would really suit the Hardelots. But why not, by God, why not?' she murmured, imagining a house in Paris. She could live with her daughter . . .

'You say he's about forty?'

'Yes, but he doesn't look it.'

'Is he in good health?'

'You know old Mr Lumbres, don't you? He's about the same age as my father-in-law. Strong as an ox.'

'We'll have to see,' murmured Madame Florent, deep in thought. 'We'll have to see.'

Some light clouds covered the sun. The ladies felt cold.

'Shall we head back? That swim was so refreshing.'

'Extremely invigorating,' replied Madame Hardelot, her teeth chattering.

They came out of the water. Their black wool swimming costumes had been designed to hide a woman's natural shape as much as possible. Both ladies seemed to be wearing sacks, but the wind billowed beneath the wet material, inflating and deflating it; bizarre, hideous protuberances ballooned up around their busts and hips. They began to get undressed. Neither of them spoke. Slowly the horse dragged the caravan back. The two women knew, even without conferring, that the introduction would be made at Pierre and Simone's engagement dinner. All introductions of this kind were arranged at someone else's marriage or engagement; it was only natural. In this peaceful province, where no one ever held dances, such solemn occasions were like county fairs, where everyone brought along the thing they wanted to sell.

'That's not how I was married,' thought Madame Florent.

It was true that she'd had to give lessons to earn a living; she was left an orphan at a very early age, after her family had lost everything and died. She taught singing and dreamed of going on the stage, but then she had met Florent, at one of her pupil's houses . . . She thought with some satisfaction of how she hadn't wasted any time, not her. She'd planned it well, winning over and marrying Florent quick as you like. At the time, she'd thought her marriage opportune and a great success. Now, she thought, 'Ha! With my hair and figure, I could have done better!' But it was no longer about her. She stifled a little sigh.

The caravan left the waves behind, taking its habitual route along the sandy path lined with wild carnations. Charles Hardelot, standing on a sand dune, proudly displayed his net, full of prawns. He walked over to the ladies and helped them down. They were wearing long white cotton piqué skirts, straw hats and thick veils to protect themselves from the sun. They opened their parasols. Simone and Agnès were sitting on the beach, doing some embroidery; Pierre was stretched out a bit further away, reading a book. Serene, benevolent, full of wisdom and peace, as confident as goddesses who hold the destiny of mortals in their hands, the two mothers walked over to the young people, stumbling a little in the sand on their high heels.

# 3

The engagement dinner began early, on a clear September evening. From where she sat, Agnès could see the garden, modest yet exquisitely proportioned and still visible in the half-light. All the windows were open and you could smell the scent of the final roses of summer. There was a basket of white roses on the table, along with the embroidered tablecloth, the heavy, gleaming Baccarat crystal and the best china, as delicate as eggshell. All the great and good of Saint-Elme had been invited. The long tables, arranged in a semicircle, occupied the entire ground floor – the drawing room, dining room, as well as part of the corridor with its black and white tiles. In the centre, in pride of place, were the fiancés, Pierre in a dark suit and Simone in a candy-pink dress. Their families surrounded them (the Charles Hardelots, the Hardelot-Arques, the Hardelot-Demestres, the Renaudins, relatives of Simone), forming a kind of guard of honour, a solid barricade mounted by wealthy men with large, healthy bodies who had invested in government bonds and intended to protect the young people from the pitfalls of destiny, and their own desires, for ever.

Tall, heavy, strong, ruddy-cheeked, they all looked alike; for generations they had been united in marriage. Whether they were farmers or landowners, they had a shared heritage, right down to

Dr Lumbres, with his enormous forehead, wide mouth and the red hair common in the region: they all came from Saint-Elme, from this ancient land, which for centuries had been cultivated with their sweat and blood. They had the hands of workmen and those enormous feet that seem designed to trample and level the earth. Compared to them, Pierre looked almost frail. His body had not inherited their vigour, but it was present in his lively, passionate gestures, in his piercing expression, in his nervous energy. Agnès remembered their childhood games: Pierre, always agile and happy, beat all the competition at running and swimming. He had never been handsome, but how supple he was, how quickly he moved . . . And then there was the lightness of his step, the fire in his eyes, and his health, good nature and charm. No one on earth was his equal, thought Agnès. But then, remembering that he was engaged, watching him standing next to Simone and seeing nearby the man who was intended for her, she scolded herself for having such improper desires, such illicit thoughts.

'I'll marry the doctor,' she thought, 'and I'll move far away. I'll never see him again. It's better that way. It's the wisest thing to do. I'll forget all about him.'

The substantial meal lasted a long time; it had been ordered from the neighbouring town, even though the Hardelots' food was always excellent. But that was how it had to be done. For a special occasion, it was obligatory to serve cold salmon and it wasn't enough for it just to be good; it had to be decorated in a way that was impossible to achieve at home: tarragon leaves, lobster tails, crescent-shaped truffles and tartlets filled with pink mousse and mushrooms were all arranged in designs as complicated as the patterns on lace. It was the same for the roast meat and the chicken, for the desserts and ice cream. Waiters with moustaches, dressed in white jackets, hired for the day, poured fine wines, brought out the various dishes and sauces. From their vantage point, Pierre and Simone could survey the majestic sight: the laden table, the drawing room whose slipcovers had been removed and, beyond, Saint-Elme's one street whose every stone they knew by heart. On this street the Hardelots were masters, kings. At one end was their factory, at the other the home of the elderly Monsieur Hardelot, and in between the houses of Charles Hardelot, the Hardelot-Arques and the Hardelot-Demestres, all in a row, all alike: shutters closed, except on days when they had guests, a little garden at the back, a glass shade over an electric light bulb, an arbour and a vegetable garden. Only old Hardelot had allowed himself the luxury of a pond and two swans. Beyond this street lived a few families not related to the Hardelots, but no one paid any attention to them; it was almost as if they didn't exist. It was like horses and cows, who can live side by side in the same field for their entire lives without seeming to notice each other.

Now night was falling; the garden paths and the little grey street were no longer visible. The lamps were lit above the table, casting their light over the peaceful faces below, flushed by all the food and the heat in the room. Sitting opposite the fiancés, keeping an eye on them, was old Julien Hardelot, with his white moustache and cropped hair, his strong, tanned hands placed squarely on either side of his dinner plate. He had come from a family of farmers, but wanted for nothing now. He was rich, respected; in his mind, these two sources of happiness merged into one. One was meaningless without the other, yet they were both of equal worth. If he had been honourable and poor, or rich and dishonest, his life would have been a failure. But he knew exactly how wealthy he was; he was aware of the integrity of his conscience. And so an extraordinary feeling of stability and security filled his soul. He was sure of himself and sure of everything around him: his house was solid, well built, set securely on its foundations; his factory was thriving; his family was obedient; his money invested in government stocks. His universe was small; he had never left France, rarely travelled beyond the borders of his own province, but he knew this little corner of earth as well as he knew his own heart. He knew what the children, the workers, the farmers were thinking and doing. And he knew what they would think and do tomorrow. Everything was calm and indestructible, within him and around him. He could calculate how much money he would have the following month or the next year, what the figures would be for the factory in ten or twenty years' time, in 1920 or 1930. He himself would be dead and buried by then. But here on earth, everything would remain the same. Until the end of time, the Hardelots would continue to furnish the businesses of the Pas-de-Calais and the north with their stationery: with their incomparably superior fine-white paper, to be used for writing – ruled in any way you needed – or for printing; their imitation Japanese paper; their Bristol Board, both white and coloured . . . They would buy land, see their children marry, save their money and die in their beds. Not the slightest doubt or anxiety would trouble their minds.

They were toasting the health of the happy couple. Charles Hardelot had lost his spectacles and was nervously feeling around among the glasses for his gold-rimmed crystal champagne flute. He finally found it, took a sip of champagne and felt filled with joy, a sweet, innocent kind of joy. Madame Hardelot raised her glass, holding out her little finger as she did so. 'She has such provincial airs and graces,' Madame Florent thought bitterly. 'And she says "Do be seated" instead of "Please sit down".' Old Hardelot drank quickly and with indifference: he only really liked beer. By now the young couple should have sipped their champagne, smiled and thanked everyone with a little nod; traditionally the young woman blushed while the young man looked at her with love and respect. But Pierre, his mouth tight and face drawn, didn't seem to be aware of what was happening around him.

Simone gently nudged him under the table. 'Pierre, aren't you going to join in the toast?' she asked.

He grabbed his glass, brought it to his lips, then put it back down so brusquely that it broke. Simone let out a little cry.

'You can be very clumsy, my poor darling,' Madame Hardelot said with annoyance.

'A broken glass means good luck,' Madame Florent sang out.

Everyone rose from the table. Charles Hardelot walked behind his wife, tripping over the train of her long dress without realising it.

'It reminds me of our engagement, Marthe . . .' he said several times. 'We've been so happy together. Let's hope that our children will be too . . .'

'But of course they will. Why shouldn't they be?' replied Madame Hardelot with a shrug.

Everyone went out into the garden. The autumn evening was peaceful and still warm. The betrothed couple led the way. They walked ahead in silence. A few minutes later Simone went inside, leaving Pierre alone. It was dark now. He walked towards the arbour, knowing he would find Agnès there. They never agreed to meet: it was pointless. It was always instinct that brought them together. On several occasions they had managed to spend a few moments alone, away from their parents. But nothing they had said was of any consequence; they were afraid of themselves. On this evening, when Pierre went over to Agnès, they were both too upset, too anxious to lie to each other. Agnès was crying.

Pierre took her hand. 'Are you going to marry Dr Lumbres?' he asked, for the idea had been torturing him all evening, arousing within him a kind of jealousy he had never felt before: he had been so sure of her.

'I have no choice. You're going to marry Simone, aren't you?' And then she added more softly, 'It will be the same type of marriage.'

At that very moment they heard Madame Hardelot's voice calling her son from the top of the steps.

'Where are you, Pierre? Come back inside, quickly, darling, your fiancée is looking for you.'

Pierre made an irritated gesture. 'They're all so annoying. They don't even know me. I have my own mind, on top of my own shoulders and I know what I want. Agnès, don't go! Don't be afraid.'

But she was trembling, trying to pull away from him.

'I don't want anyone to see me with you. I don't want anyone to find us here,' she kept saying.

'But I need to talk to you. Can I come to your house?'

She shook her head.

'Because of Madame Florent?'

'It's not that,' she whispered. 'You know very well that between the servants, the neighbours, anyone passing by . . . All of Saint-Elme would know by the next day.'

'Well, where could we meet, then? You must think of something. Girls are good at that kind of thing,' he said in the lively, slightly mocking voice he had used to tease her when they were children. She could feel her heart melting as she remembered. Yes, within her chest she could feel something becoming as heavy and fragile as a ripe peach. The sensation was so sweet, so new to her that she fell silent for a moment, then said loudly, 'I'll do whatever you want.' Her voice was surprisingly clear and distinct.

'Tomorrow, then. In the Coudre Woods. Late afternoon. Could you meet me there?'

'Yes, now go.'

'But you'll come, won't you? You will come? How will you manage it?'

'I don't know. I'll ask if I can go and see my old nanny who lives near there. Mama will take me over and come to collect me, but in between . . . I don't know, I'll have to see . . . Now go. I promise I'll be there. But why? What good will it do? It won't change anything. I'll marry the doctor and you'll . . .'

'Oh, we're no better than children,' cried Pierre. 'We've allowed ourselves to be led about and manipulated like children. And now, as I know just as well as you, it's too late. It would cause a terrible scandal. And our families would never . . . If it were only them, then . . . but grandfather would never . . . Perhaps it would be better if you didn't come tomorrow, Agnès. Perhaps it would be better if we just said goodbye for ever, here and now.'

'No,' she whispered, bursting into tears.

'Then we'll say goodbye tomorrow, all right, Agnès? Tomorrow . . .' he said, his voice growing weaker.

In the darkness he pulled her tight against him, but dared not kiss her. They stood close together like that for a moment, their hearts pounding, then, in silence, they parted.

# 4

A month later, one Sunday after Vespers, Madame Florent rang the Hardelots' doorbell. She had spent a long time thinking about what to wear and her outfit was simple but not excessively modest, formal but not austere. She had on a rust-coloured coat with black braiding and a cloche hat decorated with jet beads. She held her umbrella tightly in one hand, her handbag in the other. It was a dismal autumn day. It had rained continuously for forty-eight hours; the duck pond on the corner was spilling over. The inhabitants of Saint-Elme were hidden away behind their closed windows, drowsy from their idleness, still digesting Sunday lunch and dozing off as they watched the falling rain. Madame Florent knew that everyone could see her and she didn't mind a bit. 'At this point', she thought, struggling with her umbrella in the wind, 'there's nothing left to hide. On the contrary, a scandal might be just the thing we need to break off Pierre Hardelot's engagement. In any case we'll have to see; I'm just doing my duty as a mother.'

She went inside the Hardelots' house and asked to see Madame.

'Madame or Monsieur, preferably both of them, it's a matter of some urgency,' she said to the maid.

She was shown into the sad, cold drawing room, whose furniture had the slipcovers back on; a vase of Honesty decorated the mantelpiece while, on the piano, there was a bouquet of artificial roses. Madame Florent smiled scornfully. 'Oh, I'll never get used to this provincial place . . .'

She heard Madame Hardelot's heavy footsteps. She took a few steps forward; the door opened. The two women shook hands, half-heartedly murmuring some cold pleasantries.

'Do be seated,' said Madame Hardelot, pointing to a stiff armchair upholstered in twill. 'You told the maid it was a matter of some urgency. I must admit it gave me a fright. My husband will be here in a moment. Would his presence be . . . ?'

'Preferable? Yes, it would,' said Madame Florent, who had lost all her confidence by now and had started shaking slightly. 'I have come about a delicate and distressing matter, but I am a mother first and foremost. We are both mothers and should be able to sympathise with one another and . . . to sum it up, this is what is happening: Dr Lumbres, as you know, my daughter's intended . . .'

'Of course I know all about it. I was the one who arranged the marriage.'

'Yes, just so, it was here in your house that we met him for the first time. He seemed truly impressed by Agnès's looks and personality. In a word, he asked me for her hand; their engagement was to be made official. Now it has been broken off.'

'Broken off? But why?'

'Because, apparently, he found out that my daughter . . . your son, rather, Monsieur Pierre, arranged to meet Agnès secretly on several occasions in the Coudre Woods.'

'That is impossible,' said Madame Hardelot, stunned. 'Pierre is engaged.'

'I know he is and that is what makes the matter so serious. You realise that Dr Lumbres was made aware of this by evil gossip. Agnès has no father. It is my duty to come and ask what you intend to do about it, what intentions Monsieur Pierre has towards my daughter. Because, after all, we're not talking about some little servant,' she exclaimed (she had gradually recovered her composure and become bolder), 'we're talking about a young woman from a good family.'

'Well, Madame, a young woman from a good family doesn't agree to secret assignations,' Madame Hardelot said bitterly.

'I agree. There must have been a great deal of love, some very sincere beseeching or promises made to persuade my daughter . . .'

'Promises? That's impossible! But you know as well as I do that he's engaged.'

'He wouldn't be the first man to . . .'

'Such things do not happen in *our* family,' Madame Hardelot said haughtily. 'Pierre made no promises, of that I am certain. Your daughter must have been chasing him.'

'What are you saying, Madame?'

'I know exactly what I'm saying, Madame.'

They both had stood up and were glaring at each other with hatred. Madame Hardelot was the first to regain her composure.

'This is serious, very serious indeed. This is something a man must consider. Charles! Charles!' She opened the door and called out, 'Josephine, my dear, please ask Monsieur to come.'

In silence, they waited for the man, the judge, to arrive. He came in.

'Charles,' Madame Hardelot blurted out, her voice quivering with emotion, 'Madame is saying, is claiming . . . that Pierre made certain promises to her daughter, in the Coudre Woods.'

'What sort of promises?' asked Charles harshly.

'But . . . to marry her, naturally.'

All three fell silent.

'This is disastrous,' Charles said at last.

His wife was crying softly, her face hidden in a handkerchief.

'I know Pierre. If he finds out that Agnès has been compromised, that her engagement has been broken off, he'll want to marry her. He has always loved her. Oh yes, I knew that very well. But why didn't you keep an eye on your daughter? This is such a scandal. We've set the date for the wedding. The invitations have already been ordered. He has to marry Simone!'

'But what about my daughter, what about her?'

'Oh, I don't give a damn about your daughter,' said Madame Hardelot, forgetting all her manners. 'All she had to do was resist.'

'Marthe!' cried Charles, 'Marthe! I beg of you, ladies, please don't say things you will regret. We love our children. We want them to be happy. We must think. Think a great deal and say very little.'

'I'm warning you,' said Madame Florent, 'Simone will find out about her fiancé's behaviour. You know very well that such a thing could never remain a secret in a tiny little place like Saint-Elme. What will she think? She'll see very clearly that he's only marrying her for her money. Of course such things are tacitly understood, but young women do not see life as we do. You told me yourself that she wasn't always easy-going. What kind of future are you planning for Pierre?'

She paused for a moment, then added more softly, 'Granted, Agnès doesn't have the kind of money Simone has, but she's not completely poverty-stricken. Her father left her a dowry made up of very safe stocks and Russian bonds.'

Charles had removed his spectacles; he wiped the lenses, put them back on, then took them off again, obviously upset.

'Hear me out, Madame. I'm going to tell you my honest feelings and I am certain that my wife will agree. If it were only up to us . . . we love Pierre so much. But it isn't only up to us. His marriage was arranged by my father. You know him. You know that he has never allowed me my own money, that I'm not even a partner in his business, just a sort of unpaid employee. He gives me a living allowance and he'll give one to Pierre if he approves of whom he marries. What can I say? He's old. He is . . . let us call a spade a spade, tyrannical. I have never questioned his will. I have always believed, as Clemenceau did of the French Revolution, that the family is an institution that one must accept as a whole. Pierre should do as I do. What's more, he's twenty-four. His future in the factory will be guaranteed. But if Pierre goes against his grandfather's will, who knows what disasters might follow, for his grandfather will not allow him to remain here after the kind of scandal that you're talking about. Finally, are you sure, ladies, that what you are getting yourselves all worked up over isn't merely a matter of gossip and slander?'

'Yes, perhaps that's all it is,' exclaimed Madame Hardelot. 'There's nothing for it, Charles, I'm going to ask Pierre to come in. What do you think?'

'Be careful. This is a delicate situation.'

'No, I want my mind put at rest. He's being accused, he has the right to defend himself. It's the least we can do.'

'Be careful not to arouse the suspicion of the servants, Marthe. Josephine has already given me an odd look.'

'Really?' asked Madame Hardelot, upset. 'Tomorrow I'll let her go. And anyway, I suspect she's seeing Papa's driver . . .'

'That's awful. If Papa had the slightest suspicion . . .'

'Certain people,' said Madame Hardelot, glaring in fury at the other mother, 'certain people couldn't care less about the catastrophes they cause.'

'You have the nerve to say that to me? To *me*? When my daughter's entire future . . .'

All three of them suddenly stopped speaking.

Pierre had just come in. 'I can hear you from my room. At least, I heard my name and Agnès's. What's going on?'

He forced himself to remain calm; he said hello to Madame Florent.

'This woman,' cried Madame Hardelot, 'claims that you enticed her daughter into the Coudre Woods. What *I* say, is . . .'

'It's true, isn't it?' asked Madame Florent softly.

'We met twice. Both times in the presence of Agnès's old nanny. Agnès and I wanted to say goodbye. We were both promised to others. I had given my word and we agreed to part. You are the ones who have brought us back together, for if the least harm happens to her . . .'

'She's ruined!' cried out Madame Florent, raising the umbrella and handbag that she had held tightly against her heart in a gesture of despair reminiscent of Tosca when, in the last act of the opera, the heroine throws herself on the lifeless body of her lover. It surged forth from the depths of her memory, from a time when she dreamed of going on the stage and would spend her evenings singing the great operatic arias in front of the mirror.

'Her reputation is ruined! Dr Lumbres . . . Oh, the letter he sent me . . . If my darling's father were still alive, he would slap the face of any man who dared write me such a letter. But then again, what should I have expected from the son of a watchmaker? But you, Pierre, my darling Pierre, please allow me to call you that, you who used to come to my house when you were a little boy . . .'

'Don't listen to her,' Madame Hardelot whispered in Pierre's ear, 'she's a scheming woman.'

'Madame,' said Pierre very quickly, 'may I have the honour of asking you for your daughter's hand in marriage.' He had gone completely white; he looked defiantly at his parents.

Both women let out a cry. While Madame Florent nodded 'yes, yes' and started sobbing, Charles and Marthe groaned, 'Are you mad? Do you realise what you're doing? It's not as if you took advantage of her innocence . . . You were foolish, but it's a far cry from that to . . . Pierre, your grandfather will send you away. You'll have no job, no money. You know we're not in a position to help you. And what about Simone? Are you considering Simone?'

'No,' replied Pierre, 'I'm not.'

'But what about us, are you considering us? The pain you're causing us?'

They continued shouting at him, pleading with him, but all in vain. He replied as a respectful son should; he consoled them; he tried to calm them.

But they realised it was over, that he didn't belong to them any more. Madame Hardelot's heart was breaking. She was confused and thought, 'After I've loved him so much, protected him from everything, made sure nothing bad ever happened to him, now, in the space of a second, someone has taken him from me. He won't be able to stay in Saint-Elme. His grandfather wouldn't allow it. I've lost him. With Simone, he would have lived here. I would have seen him every day. But now . . .' She wasn't even listening to the conversation between Charles and her son any more. She knew for certain that it was quite pointless, that they were losing him. His grandfather wouldn't be able to convince him either. Oh, why wasn't he docile and timorous like Charles? But in spite of herself, she admired him. 'At least he's a man, a real man,' she thought. And it was that respect, that admiration for Pierre's character that finally eased her soul somewhat. She continued crying, but without bitterness, only with pained resignation.

Later on, when she and Charles were alone, they looked at each other sadly.

'*You* wouldn't have done what he's done,' said Madame Hardelot and Charles didn't know (nor did she) whether she was criticising him or praising him.

Charles sighed.

'Do you think they'll be happy together?' she asked, after a moment's silence.

Charles had absolutely no idea.

'Ah, my darling,' he said finally and, with a gentle, hesitant gesture, he stroked his wife's forehead and grey hair. 'All this is very painful to me . . . No, not just how badly these two children have behaved and all the problems I can see ahead (for, naturally, my father will hold me responsible for everything – but then again, I'm used to that). None of that matters. No, it doesn't,' he continued, seeing Madame Hardelot's surprise. 'If he had married Simone, it would have changed nothing. Whether you have an arranged marriage or not, life is always . . . very long . . . I place the happiness of these children in the hands of Providence, but I know how fate defines happiness, in its divine wisdom: worry, anxiety, endurance, our worldly goods, Marthe . . . We two have been happy, but I can still remember the early years and our first night together, when you cried . . .'

'Don't be so silly,' Madame Hardelot said softly, through her tears.

'My father's temper and how you fought with poor Mama, and when Pierre was born, and two years ago when you were ill and needed that operation. Now we're facing old age and the marriage of our child . . .'

He was speaking quietly, whispering broken words, as if in a dream.

'The day I asked you to marry me, the seed of it all was there. And what lies in store for them? Ah, ask the maid to bring me a nice warm cup of camomile tea, will you, Marthe? I don't know what's the matter with me. I'm having trouble digesting my food.' He rubbed the spot between his stomach and his heart. 'All of this, you know, all of this . . .'

He fell silent. Madame Hardelot wiped her eyes and went into the kitchen to ask for the tea. She didn't understand what Charles was feeling; she was irritated and upset. She couldn't see beyond tomorrow and the scene her father-in-law would make, and then Pierre's wedding, which would have to be very small and private if Julien Hardelot refused to attend. The rest belonged to the world of men.

# 5

They were coming out of the church: the newlyweds, their parents and the witnesses. It was a small group, made up of people who felt sad and lost on this Parisian street, beneath the rain. Monsieur and Madame Hardelot had been driven to near distraction by the stubbornness of Julien Hardelot, who refused to see his grandson, and by Pierre's determination to get married as soon as it was legally possible, ignoring his mother's advice ('Just wait a while ... Everything will sort itself out. Good things come to those who wait ...'). To Madame Hardelot, this wedding in Paris was a disgrace, a scandal, but what else could they do? She didn't feel she could face the people of Saint-Elme, the congratulations of her friends. And Simone's presence there made things even more difficult. So they had conferred an imaginary relative upon Agnès: an elderly woman who lived in Paris, who couldn't travel and demanded that the wedding take place in the capital. The newly-weds would spend three months with her, said the Hardelots. 'Afterwards, we'll see,' thought Marthe, who still had hopes that everything would work out and that her father-in-law would see reason. All of Saint-Elme knew that the Hardelots were lying, and the Hardelots knew that all of Saint-Elme knew, but they had to keep up appearances.

It was a November day; the skies wept softly; the wind danced in the bride's veil; the carriages crushed the last reddish leaves. What a shame that there was to be no reception, no 'buffet luncheon' thought the two mothers with deep, sorrowful regret. Each of them believed that her own child had been sacrificed in this marriage and that never had two people been united under such sad circumstances. Madame Florent was bitterly disappointed. Right up until the very last moment she had expected the classic theatrical ending, the kind that happens in books and on the stage: the grandfather softening, opening his arms and showering his grandson with great wealth. But the horrible old man was obstinate. 'We'll have to be patient and wait until they have their first child,' thought Madame Florent, who was resolute and optimistic by nature. But for now, Agnès's small dowry and the savings that the Hardelots had given to their son were all the young couple had in the world. Pierre was abandoning hope of any legacy. The thought that he had been snatched away from the factory, from Saint-Elme, made his mother miserable, and especially the idea that he could possibly be happy so far away from her.

Happy? Were the young couple happy now? They had eaten lunch in the little pied-à-terre rented by Madame Florent; they had changed their clothes; they had leaned forward so their relatives could kiss them. They had listened to their familiar voices, so sweet despite the hint of bitterness that comes with maturity (just as milk turns sour with age): 'As long as you have no regrets, my darling ... Never forget everything he has sacrificed for you ...' They were alone.

They were to spend their first night together in a hotel. They were embarrassed, ashamed of the shiny new wedding rings, of the fact that they were so obviously newlyweds. Pierre couldn't help thinking about his grandfather's country house, just outside Saint-Elme, where his parents had spent their honeymoon and where he would have taken his new wife if everything had gone to plan . . . if everything had been different . . . He didn't like this hotel room. They had picked it at random; it was an old, luxurious hotel on the Avenue de l'Opéra. They were used to the silence of Saint-Elme, so the noise of cars, the voices in the corridors, the sounds from the street, made them shudder nervously. Their desire for each other was paralysed by the emotions of the day, the strangeness of the place, exhaustion.

Never had they felt less in love. They had no regrets, of course, but Pierre thought, 'With Simone, everything would have been simpler' and Agnès reflected, 'I don't know who he is any more. He's looking at me so coldly. He's like a stranger.' She felt cold. The brass bed, the black marble bathroom, the enormous table, everything chilled them to the bone. The shutters were closed, but the bright, strange lights of Paris seeped through them. They could feel a deep, low tremor in the walls.

'What's that?' asked Agnès, frightened.

'It's nothing,' murmured Pierre. 'It's just the Métro.'

They fell silent. He was afraid to kiss her, to touch her. Up until now they had thought of their wedding day, their wedding night, as the culmination of their love, a happy ending for them. 'But it's only just beginning,' they thought, astonished and depressed.

A little while later Pierre forced himself to talk, to laugh. For the first time he used the familiar 'tu' with his wife. His wife . . . But he scarcely recognised her. She was wearing a dress he'd never seen before and had a new hairstyle. Then, suddenly, everything changed. Sitting in front of the mirror, she took out her hairpins. He felt bolder at once, whispered her name several times, kissed her hair, her lips; he desired her. She waited, docile, trembling, anxious.

It was dark when he woke up. He climbed out of bed, switched on the lamp and leaned over his wife. She was sleeping. She had covered her eyes with her arm when he had gone over to her and had kept that childlike gesture as she slept. He studied her with such sweet, profound happiness that he said out loud, into the silence, 'How wonderful this is, my God, how wonderful everything is.' Shyly, he stroked her bare shoulder and slender arm. It was less a caress than a tender attempt to engrave a memory of her, just as she was that night. He might one day forget the sound of her voice, which would change with age, as would her body, her features; but he felt that the delicate outline of her body, her rather frail wrist, the fine, smooth curve of her arm, her breast rising and falling as she slept, would remain for ever imprinted in the palm of his hand. He smiled, surprised to feel so moved. He was passionate by nature; he'd had affairs. But it wasn't the physical pleasure she had given him that made him feel so strongly attached to her. It was something else, a feeling that arose in a domain more subtle than the flesh, more ardent than the soul. 'It's deep within us,' he whispered. 'It's in our blood.' He felt his own rushing faster. Never had he been so happy. He moved slightly and she opened her eyes; he sheltered her eyes with his hand and gestured for her to go back to sleep, to listen to him, not to be afraid of the dark, of this strange room, he was with her. He pressed her tightly against him and both of them fell asleep.

# 6

'Charles! Where are they? They're not coming. What time is it?'

Madame Hardelot asked the question for the tenth time; she was trembling.

She was standing out in the street, in front of her house in Saint-Elme, with no hat on. It was the height of impropriety to be seen this way, without her hat and coat at seven o'clock in the evening, with everyone able to stare at her. But for the past forty-eight hours, the world had seemed as shaky and vulnerable to collapse as the scenery in a theatre; even Saint-Elme was in a state. It was the end of July 1914. No one wanted to believe there would be war, but everyone could feel the hot breath of its approach. Pierre Hardelot was bringing his wife and son back from Spain before going to join his regiment. He was an engineer and, since his marriage, he had been sent by his company to work in Budapest for a while, then in Madrid. His parents hadn't seen him in thirty months; they had never met his child, who had been born in Spain.

'To see him again!' thought Madame Hardelot in despair. 'To see him and lose him again at the same time. But there can't be a war; it isn't possible. It simply isn't possible for such a thing to happen.' That evening, millions of people were saying the same thing. Even though they knew that every century and every country had had its share of war and misery, it seemed that, by special decree of divine Providence, *this* century, *this* country would be spared.

'Of course, Alsace and Lorraine . . . Of course, the Emperor of Germany, and the Tsar, and Serbia,' murmured Madame Hardelot. 'Of course, there's all that. But my God, we're talking about Pierre, my own son. It isn't possible. This is a nightmare.'

'Why didn't we go and meet them at the station?' she cried out reproachfully, turning towards Charles.

'But you know very well, my dear, that my father would have found out.'

'So what?' she exclaimed bitterly. 'He has the nerve to forbid me to see my son, *my own son* who's being sent to die?'

'Don't get so worked up, Marthe. Being called up is not the same as going to war. And besides, it is my profound conviction that a world war would be fought almost without any blood being spilled. Just imagine if that weren't the case, if every country sent all its forces into battle, with the terrifying progress that the arms manufacturers are making . . . Where was I? Well, yes, there would be such terrible carnage that all of civilisation would be destroyed. You can understand why no state would wish to answer to posterity for such a crime. No, all everyone will do is try to intimidate each other, I'm sure of it. In a few days the embassies will start negotiations and the cannon fire will cease.'

'Why didn't you let me go to the station?' repeated Marthe, who hadn't been listening to a word he said.

'Listen to me now; we simply cannot openly take sides with our son against our father in front of the whole town. Of course people will find it natural if your daughter-in-law and grandson pay a visit to you, but it would be unacceptable for them to stay with us. My father said so very explicitly and in front of many people (it was at cousin Adèle's birthday party), all of Saint-Elme was there . . . When someone asked him if he had any news of Pierre, he said, "He disobeyed me. He doesn't exist for me any more." What can we do, Marthe? He's in charge. They'll stay with Gabrielle Florent. You can see him as much as you like and we'll still keep up appearances. Society relies entirely on nuances.'

'And stupidity. Besides, he's leaving tomorrow.'

'My dear, you do upset me. Sometimes you say things that make you sound like . . . like an anarchist, if you'll pardon the expression.'

'Look, just leave me alone,' she shouted, then leaned against the door and started to cry. Crying in the street! How could she let herself behave like that? She didn't give a thought to what the neighbours would think, and the other busybodies. In every house that night a woman was crying and none of them cared what was happening outside her own home. Madame Hardelot stood on her doorstep, sobbing uncontrollably into her handkerchief. But a car was coming; inside were Pierre, Agnès, a child, the luggage. She could already hear Pierre's voice, tender and slightly mocking: 'What's this, Mama? Are you crying? Tears of joy, I hope? Are you happy to see us?'

She threw her arms round him and hugged him tightly. 'When are you leaving? Do you have to go right away?'

'No, not at all,' he said, as if he were talking to a child.

But she knew very well he was lying; she could tell just by looking at Agnès's sad, pale face. She could keep her son for only a few hours, perhaps overnight. Devastated, she frostily kissed her daughter-in-law and the baby.

'Look, Marthe,' said Charles, 'what a handsome boy.'

But she didn't want to look at him; she didn't want to be consoled. At that very moment only Pierre filled her heart. Every smile she gave to anyone else was stolen from Pierre.

'Come inside,' she murmured automatically. 'Dinner's getting cold. You're very late. I had some strained soup made for the baby.'

'Madame,' said Agnès, 'he's already eaten. We wanted to show him to you, but you can spend more time with him tomorrow. Mama has his bed ready at her house. The maid will come and fetch him and put him straight to sleep. He's tired.'

'Oh, very well,' said Madame Hardelot with a gesture that seemed to indicate she had swallowed as much bitterness as she could take.

'We'll come back tomorrow. We'll come back as often as you like,' Agnès said softly.

'And you'll come too, Pierre? You don't hold anything against us because of your grandfather, my darling? You know very well that . . .'

'Of course, Mama, of course I know.'

'You'll come for lunch tomorrow, won't you? I don't want to drag Agnès away from her mother the very first day, but *you'll* come,' said Madame Hardelot, clinging on to a glimmer of hope, 'you'll come, my darling, won't you? Tomorrow?'

She saw how Agnès and Pierre looked at each other.

'I can't, my poor Mama. I'm leaving.'

'But when? Tomorrow? Tomorrow morning? Well, too bad, then, you'll stay here with me tonight.'

'I'm leaving in an hour,' said Pierre, 'on the last train.'

They went into the dining room in silence.

How strange everything seemed to them this evening. They ate, they talked, yet each one of them was thinking, 'I'm dreaming . . . I'm having a terrible dream.'

'Agnès will stay here with her mother,' said Pierre. 'That way, little Guy will be near you. My position? I'll have it back after the war. I did a good job, it was going well, yes . . . Not that we were rich. I wasn't destined to be rich. I don't have grandfather's temperament, but we've been very comfortable and we've been happy. I was supposed to come back to France at the beginning of October. I intended to . . . But now all that's over, unless between now and then . . .'

'It is my profound conviction', said Charles, 'that a world war would be over quickly and fought almost without any blood being spilled. Just imagine if every country sent all its forces into battle . . .'

'You'll write to us often,' Marthe said to her son. She was desperately trying to think of something else she could say to him, some final piece of advice that would not only be an expression of her love, but something useful, practical. In the past, when he left her to go back to school, she would show him the bars of chocolate and box of biscuits tucked away under his nightshirts, and that would make her feel better; she had helped him as much as possible, making the life he faced as a man seem less harsh. But right now when he faced a life that was a thousand times harsher, demanding more courage than she could ever imagine, she was at a loss. Even his bags had been packed by someone else . . . 'It's not fair,' she thought. Yes, so many mothers were saying goodbye to their sons that night, but they'd had them close by until the very last moment, while she hadn't seen him for thirty months. Fortunately, she *knew* he would come back. Yes, despite her grief, despite the tears she had shed, a secret voice within her heart whispered that others might be killed, mutilated, wounded, taken prisoner, but *her* son would come home after the war. And that evening every mother in Saint-Elme was thinking, '*My* son will be spared . . .' Each one of them believed that a guardian angel would protect her very own Jacques, her Pierre, and no one else.

'Eat something, my darling, you haven't touched a thing,' she kept saying, watching him. To make her happy, he pretended to be very hungry; he filled his plate, but the food stuck in his throat, the meat dish particularly; he found it repugnant.

'We ate lunch late,' he said finally.

'But force yourself. Who knows when you will get your next meal?'

'Come on now, Mama, we're not going straight into battle tomorrow, don't worry.'

He put down his knife and fork, looked at the familiar dining room, the open windows, the peaceful garden, the street lit up by the moon. The sadness he was feeling was a male kind of sadness, a mixture of pride and anguish. He didn't think he would be saved, he alone among thousands of men. He could see very clearly where he was headed. In spite of everything he was calm. He just thought to himself, 'What a shame I'm not five years younger. I would have been so happy to go. But . . .'

He looked at Agnès. The clock chimed eight.

'We have to leave now,' he said, looking away from his mother, pity in his eyes. A woman's tears were so painful. At the thought of the sobbing he was about to hear, the tears she would shed, his heart sank. He was eager to be among men, to hear foul language, dirty jokes, to get drunk on the cheap wine of manly camaraderie.

'But you haven't had your coffee!' Marthe cried. 'Agnès, pour him some coffee.'

She looked back and forth between her children, wringing her hands, haggard and trembling. No one replied. She went over to her son and kissed him. She was tricked by that kiss, tricked by his presence. He was there, but he was not, because he was about to leave. She felt as if she were clinging on to a phantom, a pale shadow that she couldn't hold close, that would vanish in her arms. Yet she shed not a single tear. Her pain was too strange and too intense to allow her to cry.

All four of them spoke the calmest words possible.

'Don't be surprised if my letters get delayed . . .'

'Agnès, now you look after yourself.'

'Say goodbye to grandfather for me. Explain to him that I was only here for a moment.'

'You'll be hot tonight on the train, my poor darling.'

He barely kissed Agnès; it was quick and rather cold, thought

Marthe. It wasn't tonight, in front of their parents, that they could say goodbye to each other. The night before, alone, in the silence of their bedroom, in the warmth of their bed, they had exchanged their parting kiss, a kiss that was deep and silent; there had been no lamenting, no pointless recriminations. But now, their lips were weary and lifeless.

They went into the entrance hall and formed a circle round Pierre. Charles Hardelot, who had gone out for a moment, came back holding an open bottle of champagne. Behind him was Ludivine, the maid, with a tray of glasses.

'We're going to drink to your good health, Pierre.'

'But Papa . . .'

But he insisted on this ritual. He couldn't let his son go without making a final speech. 'I've heard so many of them,' thought Pierre with a smile. For every occasion, his father had a speech at hand: for marriages and engagements, for births, for when he went away to boarding school each year. In a flash, Pierre relived those rainy October nights in the very same entrance hall; the horse champed at the bit as they loaded on the few bags that Pierre took to school, and his father said solemnly, 'Son, you are about to enter the world of men, where study, camaraderie and competition are there for your benefit. Remember that the child is father of the man and that whatever you sow today in obedience, in esteem for your excellent teachers, in long, serious hard work, you will later reap in the form of happiness, security and respect.'

Tonight, raising his glass, Charles Hardelot said, 'I drink to your victorious return, son. When you come back home, both your family and your fellow citizens will be proud of you. The valorous soldier is the glory of society.' And he brought his glass to his lips.

They all took a sip. Gently, Pierre touched Agnès's hair, then he left.

# 7

It was the very beginning of the war, when the heart bleeds for everyone who dies, when tears are shed for each man sent to fight. Sadly, as time goes on, people get used to it all. They think only of one soldier, theirs. But at the start of a war the heart is still tender; it hasn't hardened yet. It seems tied by a thousand strings to the inhabitants of another country, or to a certain village or region . . . a region never seen, but whose very name makes the heart beat faster with anguish and hope. In Saint-Elme, where the people had only ever been malicious or indifferent towards each other, everything suddenly changed: all the families that had been enemies, divided by a thousand long-standing quarrels and the jealousy caused by status or wealth, were united. The announcement of a death, the news of a wounded soldier echoed painfully through every cold, grey house. It wouldn't last. But for a few days people no longer thought of themselves; they existed for others and that helped them carry on living.

The news about the war was not good. Not the news in the papers: only an experienced diplomat or brilliant strategist would have been able to understand the newspaper articles or 'war reports'. The news didn't come in letters either, which were scrupulously designed not to diminish the good spirits of friends and relatives.

No, it came from somewhere mysterious, carried on the wind, spread throughout the land.

'It's not going too good,' farmers would say when they ran into each other.

'Seems we're getting beat over there,' the cleaning lady would admit.

Everyone went to bed, got up, ate their meals, but they thought about the war all the time. They even dreamed about the war. And the oddest thing was that everyone could still go to bed, get up, eat and sleep, in spite of the war. People did the washing, picked fruit to make jam, ordered dinner, and Agnès played with her child. Yet one man died every second (a man who could be Pierre) in that strange and terrible place they called 'the war zone'; it had started by being very far away, but it moved closer every day. Belgium had been invaded. The enemy was pushing into northern France; the enemy was only two days away from Saint-Elme, yet in Saint-Elme nothing changed. They slept in peaceful ignorance; they hid their heads in the sand and thought they were invisible. If someone said, 'It's just that, well, they could start fighting here . . .', everyone looked at him in aston-ishment. Fighting in Saint-Elme? Don't be ridiculous! Was it conceivable that between the church and the market square, on the street where the Hardelots lived, blood might be shed and bombs fall? 'Certain things are just not possible', or so they thought.

Saint-Elme went to bed peacefully. Saint-Elme woke up in the middle of the night, in a state of panic. The Germans were coming! The Germans were there! As for who had started the rumour, where the Germans actually were, why it was necessary to leave and where they were supposed to go, no one knew. Just as they had been certain, until now, that out of all the towns in the world, Saint-Elme would be spared, so they now awoke convinced that the battle would be fought in the centre of their town, that every army on earth was heading towards the nearby canal, the church, the market square and the Hardelots' factory.

Agnès was in her bedroom; she was asleep, with her child at her side, when she was awakened by a loud banging at her door.

'We're going!'

'Where to? How?'

'I don't know. We're going. Everyone's leaving. Your in-laws are waiting for us,' replied Madame Florent.

Agnès got dressed quickly, wrapped a blanket round the child and went outside. The main street of Saint-Elme was full of people. It was a clear, mild night. From the north, the refugees were arriving, in cars, on foot, on horseback, in wagons, pushing wheel-barrows full of clothing, pulling along their cows. There were vehicles from Belgium pulled by dogs; the sheep bleated, herds of cattle plodded along. Agnès headed towards the Hardelot resi-dence. No one was there. Women rushed out of their houses, half dressed; you could hear the sound of shutters being locked, doors being closed. The poor had already left. The rich waited; they would have taken their houses and the very earth they were built on, if they could. Agnès walked up to the château (this was how people referred to old Hardelot's home). She felt frightened and determined. All of this meant nothing. Danger meant nothing. Danger brought her closer to Pierre. She felt she could under-stand him better now. She would know the meaning of words like 'cannon fire, panic, the enemy is here'. If Pierre had been in some scorching hot, faraway land, she would have loved the heat of summer and a desperate need for water, as if they were mystical signs sent to her by him that she alone could see.

The gates of the château were open. Agnès hesitated for a moment at the threshold, then went inside. Anything was possible tonight . . . It all seemed so strange, more like a dream than reality: Julien Hardelot's house, with its doors wide open, trunks and baskets sitting on the steps, Marthe carrying a pile of sheets that she threw into the car, Charles Hardelot in a bowler hat and yellow gloves, dressed as if he were making the most formal Sunday visit, topping up the oil in the car, tipping the can gently and carefully, as if it were expensive wine being poured on someone's birthday. In the large ground-floor rooms a lamp sat on a table shedding its light over a small group of tearful women, the four elderly Hardelot-Arques spinsters, who had come to take refuge with the head of the family. Saint-Elme might be surrounded by an angry wave of blood and flames rising towards it, beating against its walls, threatening to engulf it, but in the women's minds Julien Hardelot's house would be spared from the wrath pouring down on them from the heavens. The cannons were so close now that the windows and chandeliers shook every time they were fired.

'I sent Ludivine to find you, Agnès,' said Charles Hardelot. 'We have to leave. Will the child be warm enough? Where's your mother?'

'She's just coming.'

'Charles,' said Marthe, rushing towards her husband, 'Oh, my poor Charles . . .'

She grabbed his hand and squeezed it tightly.

'Your father wants to stay!' she cried.

'Well, that means there's nothing to worry about,' exclaimed the Hardelot-Arques ladies. They forgot all about the battle, the sound of the cannon, the fleeing refugees. Julien Hardelot had spoken. Even the tide obeyed him.

'But . . . but that's impossible,' said Charles, stammering the way he did when he was very upset. 'They're going to fight at the canal. We'll be right in the middle of a massacre. Is that the place for civilians, for women?'

'He's saying that I have to go.'

'By yourself? Never!'

'He wants you to go with me as far as the railway station, and then come back, Charles . . .'

'I'll speak to him,' said Charles, throwing the empty oil can down on the ground and hurrying towards the house.

'Can I do anything for you, Madame?' asked Agnès.

'Oh, my child, I don't know, I'm losing my mind. Just imagine everything we have to leave behind, our furniture, our linen, our family mementos ... I'm just throwing together what I can at random, from my house and from here,' she said, nodding towards her house in the distance and then back to the château, 'but there's so little room. Do you have any luggage?'

'Two overnight cases and the baby's things.'

'Yes. You're young. You have no memories. As for me, well, I want to take everything,' she said as she picked up a variety of objects and pressed them close to her heart before putting them down again: a photo of Pierre as a child, a silver sugar bowl, a damask and lace tablecloth.

'Let me help you,' said Agnès.

The car was already half full of the Hardelots' belongings; they boxed up more silver, the factory's accounts, a cardboard hatbox full of linen.

'There's no more room,' Agnès said at last.

Charles came back downstairs. 'Let's go.'

'But your father,' cried Marthe, 'what about your father?'

'He's staying.'

'And what about you?'

'I'll come back as soon as I've made sure everyone is in a safe place.'

'But I won't leave you,' she cried. 'I'd rather die with you.'

Julien Hardelot's face appeared in the darkened entrance hall. Agnès took a step towards him. He looked at her coldly and turned his back on her.

'Father,' cried Marthe. 'Father!'

He allowed her to cover his cheek in kisses and tears. He put up with her outburst without saying a word.

'Father, at your age . . .'

He turned and spoke to his son. 'The title deeds are in the black metal box.'

'Papa, please reconsider . . .'

'I'll expect you back tomorrow.'

'But it's dangerous . . .'

'I am staying here,' he said, stamping his foot. There was no anger in his gesture; it looked more as if he were taking possession of the land. 'I'll expect you back tomorrow,' he repeated and went back into the house. He closed the door behind him and turned the key in the lock.

Charles Hardelot helped Madame Florent, who was holding the sleeping baby, into the car, along with Agnès and his wife; they left. It was nearly dawn. The church of Saint-Elme chimed the half-hour and the familiar sound roused the Hardelot-Arques ladies, who looked at each other as if awaking from a nightmare into reality.

'I think . . .' the first one began.

'Since Julien's staying . . .' said the other.

The third one was already pulling her black shawl more tightly round her chilly shoulders, ready to hurry home. Only the fourth one, the youngest, murmured fearfully, 'It's the cannon fire that frightens me . . .'

'We'll all stay in the drawing room,' said her sister. 'Everything's so muffled in there that we won't hear a thing.'

Heads bowed, pale, proud and frail, suddenly aware of how inappropriate it was to be standing there, alone, out in the street at such an hour, they all went back to their little house that sat in the shadow cast by the château.

# 8

Simone Renaudin and an elderly relative who was her chaperone
passed the Hardelots on the road. From the windows of the two
cars the ladies leaned out and nodded awkwardly to each other.
The cars, spared from being requisitioned, were old and enormous.
Each of them tried slyly to overtake and lose the other, but as soon
as they were on the national highway they were forced into line,
one behind the other, and had to wait their turn. It was the day
after a battle had been lost. They could see the troops passing before
them in chaos: ambulances, the wounded, cars, horses, cannons
and, among them, the civilians who were fleeing – nuns from a
convent in Flanders, farmers pulling along their cows, old people
pulling carts on which were two chairs, a pine table and kitchen
utensils held in place with planks of wood. All they could do was
inch forward. Every now and again they recognised someone from
Saint-Elme in this confusing flow of people.

'I thought I saw the notary and his wife,' said Charles.

'There are the little Dubecq children, in an English carriage,
with their grandmother,' replied Madame Florent.

But all these cars disappeared while, in a kind of malicious twist
of fate, the Renaudins' car continually pulled up alongside them.
Marthe and Simone turned stiffly away from each other.

'You might almost think she was doing it on purpose,' murmured Marthe.

Then, remembering that Charles was going to leave her tomorrow, she returned to her private hell. And Pierre? Where was Pierre? She thought she saw him every time a soldier went by. She would touch her husband's hand and say shyly, 'You see that one, over there? The one who's got his arm in a sling? He looks like Pierre.'

'You see your son everywhere, my poor darling,' Charles replied.

Not a cry, not a moan rose from the crowd. They weren't even looking at the horrific, unforgettable spectacle, the scene that would one day be a page in the history of France: the first weeks of the 1914 war. Only the children stared wide-eyed at the soldiers. As for the others ... they had left their hearts behind. They thought about their homes, their fields, the shops they had given up. Marthe could picture all her treasures: the big bed where for twenty-nine years she had slept next to her husband, her linen cupboard, the fine sheets from Flanders, embroidered by nuns in Bruges, her kitchenware – copper pans, candlesticks, sparkling bowls – and the photos of Aunt Adèle at her First Communion, and Uncle Jules, ten months old, naked on a pillow. Everything was priceless. And it would all be destroyed, pillaged, looted, reduced to ashes that billowed up towards an indifferent sky.

'But if the château and the house are bombed, where will you go?' she asked her husband naïvely, for she still believed that though walls might crumble, people could survive beneath the shells; civilians had to be spared in war. How and why a bomb chose what to strike she did not know, but it seemed inconceivable that the flesh and bones of her husband, of her peace-loving Charles, could be torn apart or pulverised like the soldiers'.

'Where will you go? What did your father say?'

'That the cellars are solid, that the house could fall but we'd be safe in the cellars.'

'But it will be so damp,' cried Marthe. 'Do you at least have your flannel jacket?'

Agnès picked up her child; he had woken up crying. She kissed his hair; it was as soft as feathers; she held him tightly, close to her heart, thinking, 'I'm not going to let you see any more war.'

'You're young,' her mother-in-law had said to her. 'You have no memories.' How wrong she was. Her memories weighed down on her insistently. Her memories weren't just objects that could be replaced by similar ones, they were part of the very place where she had lived, where she and Pierre first began to love each other when they were children. This road, for example, they had been along it so many times, on bicycles or in the car, when the Hardelots had organised picnics; the town with its cathedral in the distance, where Pierre had been at boarding school; the Coudre Woods, still visible on the horizon ... all these things were sweet, dear to her, irreplaceable ... She closed her eyes and thought passion-ately, 'I'm dreaming ... This is a horrible nightmare. I'm going to wake up in our apartment in Paris, where we lived three years ago ... Oh, my God, give me back those winter days, when I'd come home from the shops, when it was raining and I'd hurry so I could arrange the flowers and light the fire in the dining room, in that old green marble fireplace we thought was so ugly ... Then Pierre would come home and we'd have dinner. Is it possible that we'll never do so again?'

Throughout the crowds, every single woman's heart bled the same way, remembering those little moments of happiness now gone. And all the individual suffering merged into a single, immense sense of anguish for the fate of France. This anguish was so great that, little by little, it blocked out everything else. Everyone was prepared to accept bereavement, tears, suffering, if only the country could be saved; but everywhere they looked, all they could see were images of chaos and crushing defeat.

In the villages they passed through, people came out on to their doorsteps. 'Are the Germans coming?' they asked.

Yes, they were coming. The Hardelots had passed the train station quite a while ago; ordinarily, this was where you got the train to Paris, but already there were no trains running; they had to keep driving.

'If the Germans take Saint-Elme,' thought Charles, 'will they let me go back tomorrow? Won't they simply cut off the north from the rest of France?' No, it was inconceivable. He was a civilian, a civilian. He could walk through armies, dodge bullets. Laws, agreements, traditions had always defended his person, his freedom and his possessions. He refused to believe that they had been abolished or were obsolete. Yet, nevertheless, they continued to move at a snail's pace along the crowded roads.

Towards midday Simone Renaudin's car tried to pass them, swerving in the process and pushing Charles Hardelot and his family into a ditch. Everyone emerged safe and sound from the wrecked bits of wood and shattered glass. Only Agnès had a cut on her forehead. The steering on Simone's car had broken and it had crashed to a halt against a tree further down the road. No one in her car had been hurt either, but the vehicle was out of commission. They had to pull out all their packages and trunks, and wait at the roadside while the driver went to get some help.

'Don't worry, ladies,' said Charles, 'someone will give us a hand. Someone will help us.'

But the confusion was becoming ever more strange and frightening. All of Belgium and northern France seemed to be heading for Paris. From every direction a wave of people in cars, with horses or on foot closed in on the broken-down vehicles.

'Let's wait a bit longer,' said Charles, refusing to give up hope. 'Let's just wait.'

The Hardelots and the Renaudins, enemies from Saint-Elme, sat at the side of the road like gypsies. Yet the habits of their good upbringing remained so strong within them that the elderly Renaudin woman and the Hardelot and Florent ladies exchanged compliments and ceremonious apologies.

'I am truly sorry for this mishap, Madame . . . It's our driver's fault.'

'Not at all. My husband is very careless. I'm always telling him . . .'

'The important thing is that no one got badly hurt.'

Only Agnès and Simone said nothing. They looked furtively at each other.

'She's too fat,' thought Agnès. 'She looks hard and conceited.'

'That boy looks rather scrawny,' thought Simone. '*I* would have given Pierre beautiful children. What has *she* given him? He fought with his family. He's been kicked out of the factory. And why? What does he see in her? She's too thin; she's got almost no hips or bust. I don't like the kind of mouth she has.'

They had brought some provisions, which they shared. Hours passed. The help they hoped for never came.

The child, who at first had roared with laughter, was getting irritable and wouldn't stop crying. He needed a bath, a crib, some fresh milk so he could fall asleep.

'We have to keep going,' Agnès said finally, when it was late afternoon. 'We have to forget about the road and follow the railway tracks until we get to a place where the trains are running again. If necessary we can spend the night at one of the level-crossing keepers' houses because it's certain there won't be a single room available in any of the villages.'

'My God, but what about the cars, the trunks?' murmured Marthe.

But she did not protest for long. She had reached that state of nervous exhaustion when you feel indifferent to everything, apart from the most immediate, instinctive comforts: a meal, a bed, some sleep. She climbed to her feet.

'Let's start walking. I agree. Are you coming?' she asked Simone.

But Simone wanted to stay and wait for the driver, who had been gone for five hours and still wasn't back. She was clutching a suitcase and a hatbox. She had placed all her valuables, family papers and wads of money in the folds of her clothing; her mother's jewellery was sewn into the lining of the hats.

'You can go with them if you like,' she said coldly to her cousin.

Agnès had pulled Guy's pram from the wreckage of the car. Into it they wedged Charles's little metal box and a few suitcases, and started walking. The wind brought the smell of distant smoke. Villages were burning. Saint-Elme, perhaps, was nothing more than ashes now. Ambulances passed by. It was dusk. Pierre might be in one of them.

They walked for a long time. The railway tracks glistened in the last rays of the setting sun. They kept walking. Agnès carried the sleeping child against her shoulder, pushed the pram, gritted her teeth and said nothing. Madame Florent put on a brave face, hopping and stumbling over every stone on the path in her high heels. For Marthe, who was fat and had heavy, sluggish legs and tiny feet, it was harder. She had to stop.

'I'd rather die,' she cried out, in tears. 'I can't walk another step. Leave me here, Charles. Leave me, my darlings. My legs simply can't carry me any more.'

Charles took her arm and said softly, 'Come now, Marthe, be strong, my poor dear. Think of what we must look like.'

He was right to appeal to her sense of bourgeois propriety. It was the only thing that could sustain her today. It was war, they had lost everything, they were dragging themselves along the road like vagabonds, but they owed it to themselves not to cry in public, not to look upset, in short, to get hold of themselves. In the same way that a good family, despite being in mourning, stands upright in the cemetery and allows indifferent people to kiss their cheeks through their black veils.

'Think of what we must look like,' Marthe automatically repeated.

She adjusted her hat over her grey hair and, holding Charles's hand, continued walking along the railway tracks that gleamed only faintly in the darkness; her brief moment of weakness overcome, she pursed her lips, forced herself not to think about Pierre, or Saint-Elme, or her house, or her varicose veins and just kept walking.

# 9

It was night. Simone hadn't budged. Her cousin had left with the Hardelots. The driver hadn't come back. She was alone; she was still waiting. Nothing could have made her leave. She was fiercely determined, as if she were defying Agnès, who had gone. She, Simone Renaudin, would not give in, would not allow destiny to get the better of her; she would rescue herself and her possessions from disaster. One day Pierre would regret not having married *her*; no one knew what she was capable of yet. She was young; she had always led a pampered existence, sheltered from any danger, but she felt within her all the strength and energy of her heritage. Oh, if only Pierre had married her . . . Old Hardelot would have been happy to have her as a daughter-in-law. She would have helped him run the factory while Pierre was away. She would have saved everything, protected everything, for Pierre. God, how she had loved him. No one had suspected, fortunately. People saw nothing in their engagement but an arrangement between two families. But she had loved him fiercely, jealously, passionately, emotions she kept well hidden deep in her heart, beneath the heavy, impassionate façade of her plump flesh and pale complexion. She wouldn't have been afraid to stay in Saint-Elme during the bombing. She would have stood up to the Germans.

Sitting on the bank at the side of the road, with strange bright lights piercing the darkness, she listened to the confusion of voices and footsteps, the sound of heavy tyres and galloping horses. One of them, with no rider, passed so close to her that she could feel its breath right on her face. More followed, carrying wounded soldiers who still had enough strength to sit up in a saddle and look for their comrades. Other soldiers were on foot. She saw one of them walk laboriously towards her; he was dragging his leg and spoke with a breathless, husky voice. 'You wouldn't happen to have any water or wine, would you, Madame?'

'Yes, I do, wait,' she said, looking for the bottle of beer that the driver had hidden next to him before leaving Saint-Elme. 'Oh, it's been broken. We were in an accident,' she said, as she felt the jagged neck of the bottle. 'I'm terribly sorry . . .'

'Never mind,' he said automatically. He took a few more steps and fell, almost straight into Simone's arms.

'Are you hurt?' she asked.

'Yes. My shoulder.'

'Wait a moment,' she said, rifling through the Hardelots' car. She finally unearthed a bottle of milk they had prepared for baby Guy. Miraculously, it was intact. She turned on her torch, shining the light towards the soldier's face: he was a young man, covered in dirt, with the same look of exhaustion and suffering that everyone had that night. He drank eagerly, then fell back on to the bank, drained.

'Are you hungry?' she asked.

He opened his eyes, dark eyes that sparkled beneath the torch-light. 'Am I hungry! Do you have anything to eat?'

'I must have some food left.'

She found some sandwiches and a peach; he wolfed them down. Then he stretched out next to her, gazing distractedly at the dark road.

'Where are you from?' she asked.

'Cateau.'

'Have they been fighting there?'

He nodded.

'That's near Saint-Elme,' she said anxiously. 'Have . . . have the Germans crossed the canal? They have? It's just that I'm from Saint-Elme.'

'The Germans will be there by now.'

She winced.

'Do you have family there, Madame?'

'It's Mademoiselle,' she replied automatically, 'Mademoiselle Renaudin.'

'Mademoiselle Renaudin from Saint-Elme,' he repeated. 'So you got away?'

'Yes, during the night.'

'Where are you going?'

'To Paris.'

'I'm a Parisian,' he said. 'My name is Burgères, Roland Burgères.'

The food and few minutes of rest had done him good. His voice sounded livelier. She listened and looked at him with curiosity. It was the first time in her life she found herself alone like this, sitting next to a man. At first, she hadn't thought of him as a man, but as an anonymous soldier who had appeared out of the darkness, weary, wounded, dying of hunger; he was part of the ever-changing, confusing chaos that surrounded her. But now, a vague sensation took hold of her. It was night. And, even in the midst of a crowd, they were alone. He was a man; she could see his white teeth gleaming; his voice, his manners were not those of the working classes. He too leaned forward, trying to make out her features in the darkness.

'If you have family in Paris,' she said, 'I could tell them that I met you and that you had managed to get away from the fighting.'

'Thank you, but I have no one.'

'You're not married?'

'No,' he replied, smiling, 'there's no one.'

'No friends?'

'I'm not a very nice person.'

'I'm sorry. I would have been happy to do something for you.'

'You can . . . Give me your address in Paris. As soon as I can, I'll come and thank you for having fed me and looked after me. Speaking of which, do you have any cigarettes? You don't smoke? No, of course, you're a young lady from Saint-Elme . . .'

He stood up with difficulty. 'Goodbye, Mademoiselle. I'm very happy that chance brought us together in this charming setting. My injury is not serious. I doubt I'll be granted leave to convalesce. But you never know, perhaps I'll be luckier next time. Give me your address,' he said again.

'I'll be staying with one of my cousins,' she replied, quickly and quietly. 'Madame Hullin, 184 Boulevard Saint-Germain.'

'Good. I won't forget. Goodbye, Mademoiselle. And good luck.'

'Good luck to you too,' she said.

She offered him her hand. With a sudden movement, he picked up the torch she had dropped and shone it towards her face: her forehead, her mouth and her eyes, then the rest of her body. He smiled. 'Give me a kiss, for luck.'

'You're mad!' she cried, starting with fear and secret pleasure.

His voice was soft and nonchalant. 'We're at war, young lady from Saint-Elme,' he said. 'A shell could land on our heads at any moment and you would never have known what a kiss was like.' He walked towards her; she pulled away. He laughed again, took her hand and kissed it. 'Don't be afraid. The fever and exhaustion are making me feel intoxicated. Well, goodbye then. My strength is back, thanks to your excellent care. Your address in Paris is 184 Boulevard Saint-Germain, right? See you soon, Mademoiselle Renaudin. Until then!'

He picked up his bag and, dragging his leg behind him, went on his way. She sat there, breathless. The war, the defeat, all that was less real to her than this man's voice, the way he had kissed her hand. But what about Pierre? Pierre had never touched her. He had briefly kissed her forehead one evening, in front of his parents, chastely, the night of their engagement party. But tonight, the whole of her powerful body, her fiery, rapid blood, had quivered and seemed to come alive. And her weariness, the danger, increased her disturbing exhilaration. After a moment she got hold of herself.

'He doesn't seem a very serious-minded person,' she thought. 'A Parisian, with no family, no friends. Maybe he's a gold-digger. His name is Roland. That's a nice name ... Roland Burgères ... I'll never see him again,' she concluded forcefully, her hand placed over her pounding heart. Was it really her heart? This strange, profound beating seemed to come from a place she had never known existed. She sat very still, watching the stream of people all around her. There were so many men ... She was intoxicated by the living, sensual heat of all these starving, exhausted men who passed by without even glancing at her. She was ashamed of herself, but she couldn't curb her thoughts any more than she could stop the blood from flowing through her veins. At last the driver returned with a truck. They loaded the bags. They coupled the car to it. They continued on their way to Paris. It was just a few days before the Battle of the Marne.

# 10

Agnès was waiting for her husband, who was coming home from the front. They were letting her have him for six days. He'd been fighting for two years and every now and then they were granted a few hours, a few days, a few brief nights together. Then he left again. It was the same for everyone. There was nothing they could do. People draw strength from adversity and the greater the struggle, the stronger they grow. Just as she had dragged the refugees along the road without flinching, gritting her teeth, so she had dragged herself forward through 1915 and now pushed through 1916, trying to see nothing ahead but the day that was drifting away, without longing for the past, without imagining the future. She was engulfed by the profound darkness of war, a darkness from which it seemed there would be no escape, a war that would last until the end of time itself.

'But he's coming home, he's coming home tonight,' thought Agnès.

She was overcome with joy. Prayers of gratitude, tender words of love rose to her lips. Pierre, her Pierre. He would be with her in a moment. She would kiss him, hold him close; he would be smiling, warm, alive, my God, alive!

'Oh, I'm so happy,' she thought, 'I'm the happiest woman in the world.'

Everything looked bright to her: the dingy little dining room, the old faces around her. She was living in Paris with her mother and the Hardelots. Charles had never managed to get back to Saint-Elme: it was occupied by the Germans. It had been two years, now, and still they had no idea what had happened to Julien Hardelot, the house, the factory. They didn't have much money. They didn't have enough room; their apartment was too small for so many people. The two mothers bickered constantly. But none of that mattered: Pierre was coming home tonight. They didn't know exactly when he would get there. They simply had to wait. Wait, staring at the door. Wait, straining to hear the sound of the taxicabs down in the street. Waiting was both unbearable and exquisite. It brought pleasure that felt like a kind of torture. They knew he was coming, didn't they, they were sure of it. Their suffering was over. Yes, it was finally over, the horrific, incessant suffering of war. And what remained was a sense of eager impatience that burned like fire.

How sweet and pleasant everything seemed to Agnès. She loved everyone. She wanted to kiss Madame Hardelot, to stroke her father-in-law's cheek. As for her own mother, she couldn't contain herself; she grabbed her round the waist, pulled her close, pressed her cheek to hers, laughing. She went into the kitchen where the Breton maid, whom Madame Florent had hired, was beating some eggs. She asked her about her father, who was away at war. She took the bowl away from her: she wanted to prepare the dessert for Pierre herself. But a moment later she was afraid she might get her dress dirty – she was wearing a new dress. Would Pierre like it? Waves of ice and fire flooded through her entire body.

'They must think I'm mad,' she thought, running towards the entrance hall, looking at herself anxiously in the mirror. She smiled; she thought she looked pretty; her delicate face was glowing, as if lit up from inside by a pure, intense flame.

'Agnès,' called Madame Florent.

'Yes, Mother, I'm coming,' she replied. But she didn't move. She wanted to wait there, in the dark hallway, pressed against the door that was about to open. The child was asleep in the next room. This very night, an hour from now, they would lean over their child together and kiss his hair. Together! They would be together. What did it matter if it was brief, she thought to herself. What was a week to her before? Many empty, useless hours. But now ... how many smiles and tears, how much joy and sadness in the space of only six days of leave. They were living in strange, dizzying times.

Everything happened just as she had so often imagined it. Everything was exactly as in her dreams: the sound of the taxi outside, the street door banging shut, Madame Hardelot's voice quivering like an old woman's with joy and fear, then the old lift rising slowly, solemnly and, even before it reached their floor, the whole family rushing out on to the landing, calling, 'Is that you? Are you really here? Is it you, Pierre?'

Yes, it was really him. The feel of a masculine cheek against hers, rough yet gentle, Pierre's hand on her arm, his voice in her ear. Agnès felt nothing else, was oblivious to everything, forgot even the cry that had risen within her the moment she heard the taxi stop in front of the house: 'The first, wonderful moment is already gone. How quickly the rest of the time will go, my God. He'll be leaving again so soon.'

# 11

The division was waiting for the relief team. They had set up camp on a small hill, above a few ruined houses, on the site of what had formerly been a village. Only the church remained standing. Pierre could see shadows moving through the darkness: abandoned, starving cats hunted in packs amid the rubble. They weren't the only ones still there: a few old people, a few children remained, hidden from view in basements. Pierre heard the two-tone toll of the bells, announcing a gas attack. His ears were still not used to these mournful, mysterious sounds. He couldn't hear them without feeling a pang in his heart. His eyes had seen so many horrific scenes of war that no sight, however horrible, however hideous, managed to affect him, at least not in an intense, lasting way. But he couldn't get used to certain sounds. He believed that even when peace came — if it ever came — he would hear them every night in his dreams: the harsh burst of barrage fire, the whiplash of the 88s, the 75s cutting the air like scythes, the whizzing of bullets and the heavy gunfire whose rumble can be sensed coming closer, slowly, ever so slowly, until it strikes, ripping open the ground. 'Mustn't give up hope,' he thought, mocking himself. 'Another ten years or so and it will all be over.'

He found his gas mask, smelled the faint sickly odour of rubber close to his face and felt the weight of the helmet on his head. Then he went out. As always, when he was in danger but not actually in battle, he thought of Agnès. He was pleased that he had never tried to hide certain things about the war from her. All around him the other men, in their letters, or when they were on leave, kept the truth from their wives and the elderly ('What's the point? They wouldn't understand,' they told themselves). Their sense of decency was partly sincere, partly pretence. They scoffed at the mock-heroic speeches of the rearguard who believed they were punishing the civilians by not sharing details of the soldiers' daily life with them. The sensitive ones felt compassion. Pierre remembered a poor lad who had been killed two days before; half an hour before he died he'd said, 'Isn't it enough that *we're* suffering?'

'Naturally, I'd never talk about it to my mother or father,' thought Pierre, 'but Agnès, well, that's different. She has to know everything I'm feeling, just as I know everything she feels.'

Whenever he was home, he made sure there were none of the misunderstandings, the painful things that poisoned other men's leaves. She never asked stupid questions. She didn't say, 'But what are you all doing? You're not getting anywhere.' She didn't ask, like his father, whether their offensive campaign would finally bring victory next spring, nor what the Allied generals thought ('Shall I tell you what I think? We lack *furia francese*,' Charles would mutter). Agnès knew everything that affected the men, the ordinary things about the division, their daily lives. And if she didn't talk to him about the war, it wasn't out of ignorance, or indifference, but out of profound and confident wisdom. He remembered their last night together. How far away it seemed, yet only two months had passed. He had held her in his arms, taking in her light nightdress, the fine sheets, the flowers next to their bed; he had looked at the shimmer-ing heavy curtains lit up by the lamp and said softly, 'We still have all this, thank goodness . . .'

He said nothing more: he was at a loss for words. But he was thinking, 'All this, in spite of what you might think, is what is truly important. The war will end, we will all disappear, but these humble and innocent gifts will remain: the cool air, the sun, a red apple, a fire in winter, a woman, children, the life we lead each day . . . The crash and din of war all fade away. The rest endures . . . But will it endure for me, or for others?'

Yes. 'For me, or for others?' That should have been the most serious question, the only real question. Yet it wasn't. After three years at war, the instinct for individual survival, while not disappearing entirely, had grown weaker within him. At times he almost forgot who he was, his name, what he liked and what he didn't. He marched, suffered, hoped with so many others, who felt the same exhaustion, the same pain, the same hope, so that his individuality disappeared: he was no longer Pierre Hardelot. He became anonymous, to some extent, lost, just as he might be tomorrow and for ever, amid the dust and remains of so many others. On days when he was depressed, he found this feeling a bitter but inspiring consolation. 'In the end,' he mused, continuing his train of thought, 'it doesn't matter if everything remains the same for me or for anyone else. The essential thing is that it exists in and for itself. Agnès . . .' Agnès asleep, in a long pink nightdress of light material with a bit of lace round the collar and sleeves. The child sleeping beside her. 'Poor Agnès. Her life can't be easy,' he thought. Very little money, looking after the house, the squabbling mothers, so many difficult chores to do . . . What with taking care of the child, who had been the most terrible bone of contention between the two grandmothers, she couldn't be a nurse, couldn't volunteer for any charity work. He didn't mind about that. Despite having moments when he lost a sense of who he was, he retained the jealous, possessive instinct innate to middle-class husbands. In his mind Agnès should take care of him alone, and of other men only through him. He would write to her about a comrade who wanted some books, another who needed a warm sweater, someone else who hadn't had any news of his family in the occupied territories; he gave her instructions about what she should do. He loved her just as she was, willing and pure. Especially pure, as refreshing as a cool stream. He closed his eyes and thought, 'She quenches my thirst.'

He could see some lights shining in the village streets below. Mass was being celebrated in the church, amid the ruins. He had attended the evening before. The army chaplain and all the worshippers were wearing gas masks, like him; the sound of the cannon fire, the screeching of the shells merged strangely with the responses . . . He went down to the church. The local people were already there, and nothing looked more bizarre than the parishioners, wearing that strange headgear designed to protect them from a gas attack, with their rosaries in their hands.

When everyone had left he went up to the altar. He had noticed it was heaped with various surprising objects. Day was breaking; he could see more clearly now. He stood astonished. Photographs, wedding tiaras, candlesticks, ornate clocks were laid out like a sad, dusty bric-a-brac sale. At the beginning of the war the village had been occupied by the Germans, then they'd gone. The fleeing villagers had taken their most precious possessions to the church before leaving, hoping they would be safe there. Now the village had been destroyed. 'Another bombing like the one the other day,' thought Pierre, 'and you won't even be able to tell where it once stood.' But the photographs and clocks remained. Pierre walked out of the church at the very moment when a distant explosion made the old stone walls vibrate and shudder. The stained-glass windows had been shattered long ago. The soft, rosy light of an exquisite dawn spread through the church.

Pierre remembered the gas that was heading in their direction. It caused the most horrific of deaths.

Then he saw one of his men coming towards him. 'It's passed us by,' he said.

# 12

Charles Hardelot was on his way to church. For a month now, since the German attacks to the north of the Chemin des Dames on 8 February, there had been no word from Pierre. For six days, long-range cannons had been bombarding Paris. Agnès, pale, dry-eyed, shut herself away with her child. Madame Hardelot, sick with grief, stayed in her room, and Madame Florent went back and forth between the two women. Charles Hardelot was fulfilling his duties as a Christian. Dressed in black, carrying his umbrella, he made his way through the streets of Paris as if he were marching into battle, listening closely to see if he could hear the rumbling of the cannons. He was not a belligerent soul. In 1914 the *taubes*, those planes that resembled birds, had awakened a profound sense of anguish in him (though he wouldn't have admitted it to anyone) and he shuddered whenever he thought of the luminous trail of the zeppelins as they moved through the sky. He always insisted on going down into the cellars as soon as the first warning of the siren was heard.

'My poor darling,' Marthe sighed. 'We're surely more likely to get killed down there than up here with the bombs.'

'It isn't out of cowardice that we should take shelter, Marthe,' he replied, 'but to obey official orders. The strength of the army

depends on discipline. I would go so far as to say that, in times
of war, civilians make up an enormous army. Soldiers at the front
are watching us; they are watching us closely. They expect us to
set an example. The best example we can give is strict obedience.
The government has not ordered us to evacuate Paris: I stay. The
government has ordered us to take shelter: I rush down to the
cellars. This is how I understand and practise civic discipline,
Marthe, since it is the primary virtue of every citizen.'

Nevertheless, in the four years since violent death had reigned,
even Charles Hardelot had begun to come to terms with the idea
of it, telling himself that since the entire current generation was
probably destined to be struck down sooner or later, he had better
try to get used to it.

Everyone tried to think like this. 'It doesn't matter whether you
die in your bed or somewhere else,' people would say. But each
of them was really thinking, 'It will happen to someone else.'

Today, however, everything was calm. As he got closer to the
church, Charles Hardelot walked more slowly. He was forty-five
minutes early. A man excessively concerned with being on time,
he would arrive at the train station with all his luggage long before
his train had even been coupled. Or he would get to church while
the previous Mass was still being celebrated. Invited to a formal
dinner in Saint-Elme, he never failed to appear at the moment
when the lady of the house, a dressing gown thrown over her
frock, was in the pantry, overseeing the scooping out of ice cream
for dessert while the servants finished setting the table.

Looking at his watch again, he thought, 'That's funny, my watch
must be fast' and he climbed slowly, solemnly, up the steps of the
church. It was not from old Julien Hardelot that he had inherited
his religious devotion. Julien Hardelot had never gone so far as
to proclaim himself an atheist; though he wasn't himself obser-
vant, he thought religion a good idea for his wife and children.
His personal beliefs could be summed up like this: 'God may be

God, but *I'm* Julien Hardelot.' God had a well-defined place in
the spiritual realm but, where anything earthly was concerned,
Julien Hardelot was his own master. He didn't like priests; it upset
his son to remember how, sometimes, he even made jokes about
religion. Once, when Charles was a child, he told his father that
the priest had included the following holy text in his sermon: 'Do
not lay up for yourselves treasures on earth, where moth and rust
destroy and where thieves break in and steal; but lay up for yourselves treasures in heaven, where neither moth nor rust destroys
and where thieves do not break in and steal.'

'They didn't have strong coffers in Judaea . . .' Julien Hardelot
had murmured.

In the mind of Julien Hardelot, the teachings of Jesus didn't
apply to his century, the nineteenth century, a world of three-
per-cent returns, railway bonds and Russian securities.

Charles's pious zeal left him cold, and Charles sometimes thought
that it would have been better for his father's soul if he had despised
God, rather than merely being coldly indifferent to Him. Charles's
faith was humble, precise and scrupulous, occasionally mixed with
a few worldly thoughts: he felt himself more refined, more 'bourgeois' than his father; practising Catholicism was part of his duty.
And yet, more and more often during this cruel war, in church,
or at his evening prayers, Charles Hardelot felt himself becoming
detached from himself, a bit like Pierre in his trench. It seemed
to him that when he undressed, removing his pince-nez, his dark
clothes (or red-piped nightshirt), shaving his black moustache, he
was at the same time removing part of his soul, so that all that
remained of his soul was its core, the purest flame, burning at the
foot of his Creator. This never happened right away. He would
go inside the church. He would put his overcoat on a chair – properly folded, inside out – with his hat and umbrella. He would carefully kneel down, pulling his trouser legs up a bit so as not to ruin
the folds. He would whisper a prayer, but couldn't put his usual

worries out of his mind and they mingled with the sacred words. Then, little by little, he ceased to be Charles Hardelot, the good bourgeois husband and father. He found himself face to face with Christ, and God was listening to him.

It was Good Friday, in the Saint-Gervais church. The early evening service was about to begin. There was no pomp, no incense, very little light. As night fell, some of the candles were put out.

Charles knelt in his pew, beneath the covered statues of Saint Mark and Saint Luke, on his face the same look of submissive, zealous dutifulness that he used to have as a child, when he would show his father his school marks for the week; his father would be so annoyed by his expression that he would slap his face before even opening the notebook to see that, once again, Charles had come first in his class. He clasped his gloved hands and leaned them on the hymnal shelf. He asked God, without indignation, but with tender and pious distress, where his only son was, where was his Pierre. Was he still in that strange, vague, frightening place the imagination could not even conceive, the place that was called 'the front', 'the army', 'the battleground'? Was he a prisoner of war? Was he finally resting in the bosom of the Lord after the terrible exhaustion of battle? Pierre had never complained about being tired, but his father could feel it in his very bones, understood it instinctively, he who had no idea what it was like to fight. He covered his face with his hands.

'My poor child . . .' he whispered.

Then he thought of his own father. What had happened to him? Was he dead or alive? When, oh my God, when would this war end. When and how? Most importantly, how? Because it was worth suffering if France could emerge victorious. But what if it were all in vain? If all the sacrifices were pointless? 'I know, my Lord, that you desire total commitment, complete surrender to Your divine will, but I beg You to consider that this child is all I have in the world, and if no one comes out alive, if our best young men disappear, what will become of France? Already France's purest blood has been shed. The best, the strongest men are gone. Who will be left? Only fatherless, maybe homeless children, the weak and the cowardly. Please let Pierre come home. Take my life, but let Pierre come home. Lord Jesus, yes, I know; Pierre too has a son and this son will grow up, but there are so many years between him and me. It is Pierre whom I want, Pierre whom I understand, Pierre who is the best, truly, God, the best of our line. I am weak, fearful, selfish, cowardly, this is my sin, my greatest sin. Sometimes my own father (forgive me, Lord) is greedy and harsh. Pierre is better than we are. Please understand: it is not just a father who is begging You; Marthe would remind You that she brought him into the world, that she suffered for him, that he was such a beautiful little boy, my God . . . But I know that You did not spare Your own mother that pain. It is not just for us that I pray. It is in the name of France herself. Take pity on France. Give her back what remains of her young men. As for me, I am old and useless. I have lived long enough. I understand nothing of the kind of world that lies ahead. Pierre said that this will not be the last war, as we had believed, but the first in a long series of relentless wars, more cruel still. Wars and revolutions. Blood and more blood. Make it stop. As far as I'm concerned, we've had enough.' He whispered all this and truly felt that he, Charles, with his umbrella and his gloves and his black boots, was being dragged along by a dark current, pulled towards unknown shores.

The reading of the Psalms had finished. The choir of Saint-Gervais started to sing the Lamentations of Jeremiah. Charles Hardelot raised his eyes towards the large figure of Christ hidden beneath a purple cloth. He could picture the nails in his feet, his drooping body, his face full of compassion and pain. At that very moment the sky seemed to fall. A shell had struck the wall on the left-hand side of the sanctuary. It first hit one of the building's buttresses, shattering a support. As a result, one of the lateral pillars set between the spans collapsed. Then a section of the vault and the keystone itself, representing the crown of the Virgin, crashed down on to the faithful, burying them. Beneath the stone, beneath the beams, beneath the thick white dust lay the bloody, crushed remains of Charles.

# 13

It was over. The war was over. Pierre was alive. Seriously wounded, taken prisoner, he was in a hospital in Germany. News was coming through from the occupied areas. Saint-Elme had passed from one side to the other several times. The town had been destroyed. The château, the Hardelots' house, the church, the factory had all been machine-gunned and bombed, leaving nothing but charred bricks, ashes, ruins, crumbling walls where grass was already beginning to grow. There had been a battle in the cemetery. Later on, soldiers had camped in the square where the market was held, washed their clothing in the river. The dead were buried in the Coudre Woods. But old Hardelot had survived. Taken hostage, then released, sent to Douai, then to Arras, he finally got back to Saint-Elme while it was under German occupation. He had obtained permission to live in the country house he owned not far from Saint-Elme. Now, more than ever, he was master, king and oracle. He had 'suffered under the Germans'. The inhabitants saw him as a symbol of their indestructible land. The mayor, whom he had always hated, was gone, had been killed. Julien Hardelot made all the decisions, supervised everything. Saint-Elme would be rebuilt according to his instructions; everything would be the same as before. They would rebuild the same houses in the same places. The police station would once again have its Second Empire columns, the school its enormous cold corridors. At the factory, Julien Hardelot would reign supreme. Beneath him, under his command, occupying a position even more inferior than Charles, Pierre would be allowed to return.

He gave this information to Marthe, who had come back to Saint-Elme at the beginning of 1919. She told him about Charles, about the bombing of the Saint-Gervais church. The old man listened in silence; resting on the table, his strong, heavy hands trembled slightly. He started to speak, fell silent, looked out of the window at the desolate garden. He had received Marthe in the country house. The windows were broken; the columns from the terrace were lying on the yellowish patchy grass that had been eaten by the horses. The trees in the grounds and even the ones in the orchard had been cut down, to make huts for the soldiers and to use as firewood over four winters.

Julien Hardelot slowly turned to look at his daughter-in-law. 'There's nothing to be done, my girl. The young must leave this world before the old in times like these, or so it seems. You have your son.'

'Papa, won't you forgive him?'

He raised his hand to silence her. 'If he wants to come back to the factory, well . . . He wounded me deeply, but he fought a good war. I forgive him. No. Be quiet. As for *her*, I don't want to see her. I know myself. Even if I told you that I would accept her, my girl, I couldn't do it. I couldn't be civil to her. I won't receive her. But as for *him*, let him come back; I will pay him the same wages I paid his . . . I paid to poor Charles. We're going to have to work really hard now,' he said.

'But, Father, he's still a prisoner. In the meantime . . .'

'In the meantime I'll manage,' he said.

'Is it true what I've heard?' she asked timidly. 'That Simone Renaudin has got married, that she has come back to Saint-Elme and wants her husband to join the factory?'

He didn't reply. She insisted: 'Is she married?'

'Yes,' he said finally, 'she married a Monsieur Burgères.'

'But he's not from here!' she exclaimed. She was scandalised. Pierre had turned down Simone and her dowry; nevertheless, they both came from Saint-Elme. She felt frustrated by Simone's marriage to a stranger, a Parisian. And now he was going to join the Hardelots' factory that belonged, by divine right, to her and her family, and to no one else. Clearly, the old way of life had perished. But that it should be her father-in-law who dealt it the death blow confused her.

She pinched her lips, lifted her head beneath the thick crêpe veil she wore. 'Does anyone even know where this Burgères was born?' she asked. 'He has the worst reputation. He's always out at parties; he's a womaniser . . . He squandered his fortune, before the war, on young women. I know this from Simone's aunt, the one who lives in Paris and is one of the Lille Hardelots.'

'Well, now he has Simone's fortune,' the old man pointed out in a tone of voice that meant 'And you stupid people let her get away'.

He actually knew exactly who Burgères was: he had made detailed enquiries about him. Burgères was from a good Parisian family, an orphan; he had spent all his inheritance early on. Just before the war started he had nothing left. He had fought courageously. A bit of good luck had placed Simone Renaudin in his path. He wanted her dowry. He'd married her. But Simone was a sensible girl. She knew how to protect her money in every possible way. She had only one desire: to wrench her husband away from Paris, from the temptations in Paris. A position in the Hardelot factory would be a sure way of keeping him in Saint-Elme. She would invest her capital in the factory; Julien Hardelot had coveted it for years, ever since the time when Pierre, in his sailor suit, had played ball with Simone, in her short dress. That money should have come to the family, of course, an outcome that had been made impossible by Pierre's mistake. Now, at least, it could be invested in the factory. Julien Hardelot looked out at the spot where the battered factory stood, where it was now being rebuilt. He put on his hat and took his thick cane with the ebony handle. 'Come on, my girl, let's go and have a look around. Have you seen it all yet?'

'No, Father, I came straight here.'

'Come. You'll see that everything's getting back to normal. They're rebuilding everywhere.'

She followed him out. They walked down the road that separated his house from Saint-Elme. She looked around in horror. The gutted earth spewed forth its insides – a yellowish slimy mud mixed with scrap iron, boots, tins of food, wood, steel debris, all tangled up, twisted, lumped together with wood, bones and stones. Signs had been put up on the road, an arrow with writing in French and English:

VISITEZ LES CHAMPS DE BATAILLE
VISIT THE BATTLEFIELDS

On both sides of the road were the desiccated remains of trees shattered by shells; they were discoloured, poisoned in the gas attacks.

'A war that kills trees too.' Poor Marthe sighed. 'Who could have imagined it.'

But as for her father-in-law, all he could see was the factory. He walked on, his eyes fixed on the spot where it would be rebuilt. He struck the ground with his cane, moved his lips as if to speak, working things out in his mind. He wasn't expecting years of prosperity. There would be ups and downs. But that wasn't important. What truly mattered was that he could finally work again, that once more, every morning, he could go to his office, stay until noon in his little glass cubbyhole above the machinery room, supervise everything, control everything, feel he was master. What exquisite pleasure! Poor Charles had never understood that. And Pierre? He had placed a great deal of hope in Pierre, but, through his marriage, Pierre had let him down. He might forgive him, take him back in, give him back his place in the factory, but he would never trust him again. Ah, why hadn't he married Simone? She was a girl after Hardelot's heart: tough on herself and on others, thrifty, diligent. As for her husband, Roland Burgères . . . He'd got the measure of him straight away. He was pretentious and useless. She'd whip him into shape. At the factory he'd obey Hardelot. At home he'd obey Simone.

'And she'll do what I tell her to,' thought Hardelot. 'She knows what I'm made of . . . that I've got my head on my shoulders. She knows that if she trusts me to look after her interests, I'll do it as she would herself.'

And, once again, a serpent nipped at his heart at the thought that she wasn't Pierre's wife. He stopped, pointed at a small pile of pebbles on the path. 'Jault's Inn,' he said curtly.

Marthe stared in astonishment. 'Here?'

'Yes.'

'But then, where is the street, where are the houses and Dubois ladies' haberdasher's shop?'

He made a gesture as if slitting his throat. 'Razed to the ground.'

Women dressed in mourning wandered through the rubble, looking for what was left of their homes, unable to recognise them any more. Where they had once lovingly tended their gardens, only wild poppies now grew. A child ran past, tugging them out of the ground. Finally, they were on the street where the Hardelots lived. They were pulling down the ruins. Marthe saw her house, or rather, the corner of it that was left, unstable and frightening, with a hole in the wall through which she could see one of her sitting-room chairs caught in the beams.

She knew that the next day they would use dynamite to blow

up these crumbling remains that threatened to come crashing down on their heads. She stood there, motionless, looking at her house the way one looks at a dead body in an open coffin.

A busload of tourists had just gone by. Indifferent faces appeared at the windows.

'Visit the battlefields!' a guide called out. 'See where the bombs fell. This way, ladies and gentlemen.'

# 14

On 14 July in that year of victory, the day dawned cold and unsettled. A few drops of rain fell, then some pale sunlight shone through the clouds. Autumn was in the air. Crowds blocked the road; street vendors hired out ladders so people could watch the parade go by, and every folding chair, every stool, every rung cost a fortune. On the Boulevard de la Madeleine, people surrounded street singers, and the workers formed a chorus, belting out the refrain:

So we got 'em after all!

But it was strange, there was no real joy on their faces. They were thinking of all the dead, all the destruction. Yet that hadn't stopped them from being wild with joy over the Armistice. No. This was something else: France was weary and only wanted peace. Even memories of its victories were unwelcome. More than anything, its people just wanted to stop thinking about the war. Everything now seemed more interesting, more vibrant, more relevant than the war: black music, new poetry, women's short hair and short dresses, relaxed morals. 'Peace. My God, just leave us in peace. We won, well and truly,' thought the soldiers. 'Leave politics to the schemers, the profiteers, the braggarts, the thieves. *We* just want to be left in peace.' 'We've been heroes long enough,' said the oldest with a sigh. 'Give us back our wives, our homes, our good wine.' 'Give us everything the good earth can provide,' cried the young men as they returned from the grave, famished and voracious. 'Lazarus must have enjoyed a good meal after his resurrection; how well he must have slept in his warm bed. Let us eat, drink, love. As for all the rest, we've had enough.'

The crowd welcomed the parade, the soldiers, Joffre and Foch and the foreign kings, cheered them on, but in their hearts they remained sad and nervous. People said that the soldiers marching beneath the Arc de Triomphe had never actually seen combat, that, as usual, glory was reserved for some and death for the others. And, no matter where you looked, there was nothing but mourning veils and armbands, children dressed in black.

A bitter wind blustered through the flags. The English and the Americans were having a good time. From the old dirty taxis that looked as if they'd been at the Battle of the Marne, they leaned out, kissed the women. On the pavements, disabled war veterans passed by in small wheelchairs. Pierre, pale and thin, unrecognisable with his forehead and arm covered in bandages, limped slowly along, supported by Agnès; he was bumped a bit in the mêlée, not maliciously, but because no one really noticed the wounded any more. During four years of war people had got used to seeing them. They no longer aroused either admiration or affection. 'We don't rank high nowadays,' thought Pierre. 'They pity us, of course, but only superficially and because we make them feel uncomfortable. But their pity will disappear long before our wounds heal.' Like his fellow soldiers, Pierre was utterly exhausted: exhausted physically, mentally, spiritually. He didn't know what to do: return to Saint-Elme and accept old Hardelot's offer, or try to make his own way, as he'd done before the war. But everything was more difficult now than it had been in 1911.

He had gone to see his former employers.

'They've kept my job for me,' he told Agnès. 'They assured me that as far as I was concerned, nothing had changed. But I'm not as valuable to them as I used to be and they know it. Just look at me. They want to send me to Brazil, to a region that is barely civilised. "You'll be riding a lot," they said. "You're an excellent horseman."'

He stumbled a bit on the paving stones of the Rue Royale. 'That's all in the past. *I'm* all in the past.'

'Don't they have anything for you in Europe?' Agnès asked softly.

He shrugged his shoulders. 'Do you know what they told me? That Europe was too small for everyone coming back. And we thought we'd killed too many people. It seems we were wrong. It wasn't enough, apparently.'

There was dancing in the streets. On a platform draped in the French flag, a blind soldier, who was extremely young, swayed to the music in the arms of an older woman who wore too much make-up. She was leading and, when the music stopped, she held on to him and planted a long wet kiss on his mouth with her thick red lips. And the soldier, the soldier just laughed, letting himself be led through the darkness by the horrible creature. At Weber's some American officers were breaking the windows.

It was the final war. There would never be another. The thirst for blood had been satisfied. Not only was it necessary to forget the war: it had to be vilified in people's memory. People rushed towards the dance halls and restaurants. They crushed themselves into Claridge's and the Carlton dining rooms. It was evening. Dead leaves swirled about as if it were October. Above the mad, carefree and, in spite of everything, deathly sad city, above the pretence and the tears, a reddish, turbulent dusk began to fall. To attract the Americans, ordinary women and prostitutes placed widows' veils over their dyed hair, and wore dark-coloured dresses and pink stockings.

'You'll be happier in Saint-Elme,' said Agnès.

'In Saint-Elme? Impossible. You would have to be accepted by grandfather as . . .'

She interrupted with a laugh. 'How silly you are. Why would I care about that? As long as we're together, why would that even matter?' She touched his arm gently. 'I love you and nothing matters but you.'

'That may be how it seems because we were apart for so long,' he whispered.

'No. I'll feel the same way in twenty years.'

'So, we must be very happy, then?' he said with a teasing smile.

'You mean you don't think so, you ungrateful thing?'

'The past four years have been so long,' he said, 'so difficult.'

'Yes, but surely we have used up all our bad luck in one go.'

'No doubt about that,' replied Pierre. 'No one should have to pay such a price twice.'

He stopped, placed his hand over his chest. 'I'm out of breath. I can't walk any more.'

'I'll get a taxi. We'll go home.'

They returned quickly to their flat. There weren't a lot of people left on the dark streets, beneath the moonlight. Families turned on their lamps and ate their dinner, without a thought for the rest of the world. The foreigners crowded into the dance halls and restaurants. Suddenly, Paris seemed half empty. Paris seemed bled dry.

# 15

Pierre's and Agnès's second child, a girl, was born in Saint-Elme in 1920. The young Hardelots were living with Marthe. The new house had the same proportions and was in the same position as the old one. Its solid walls stood between the main street and the garden, in the shadow of the factory; it proudly displayed its glass awning above its three stone steps. But the bower was no longer there and the trees had all been felled. Beneath the sunlight, the bare garden made Madame Hardelot sigh. 'It's scorching out . . . We have no shade any more,' she said.

That summer was particularly hot. After lunch, Agnès took her two children, Guy, who was seven, and Colette, whom she was still breastfeeding, to the Coudre Woods. The baby was asleep in the pram, under a gauze cover to protect her from the flies. Guy was playing with the pine cones, wiping his dirty hands on his mother's skirt. Agnès was sewing. After an hour, Madame Hardelot appeared, with Madame Florent at her heels.

'Agnès, this child doesn't have a hat on,' Marthe remarked.

'It doesn't matter, Mother, there's no sun here.'

'There may be no sun but there's a storm brewing.'

'Look at this little girl; she laughs whenever she sees me,' said Madame Florent.

The two grandmothers looked at the baby who was waking up, waving her arms about and crying shrilly. Each of them wanted to pick her up and rock her. The same scene took place ten times a day. Agnès waved a branch to shoo away the flies and mosquitoes that were stinging her bare arms and neck. After the two grandmothers had sufficiently upset the baby, they handed her over to her mother.

'Poor little thing, she wants her mother. Don't you, my darling, my little sweetie? Calm your daughter down. You don't know what you're doing. What's wrong with her?'

'She was happily sleeping and you woke her up.'

'Me? But I didn't touch her. It's always the same. I won't go near these children any more,' said Madame Florent.

The pine needles were slippery. There was a sweet smell of decay. It was stiflingly hot. Earlier, Agnès had found a little silver ring in the Coudre Woods.

'What's that, Mama?' her son asked.

'It's mine, my darling,' she replied. 'I lost it here ten years ago. I was going for a walk with your papa . . .'

She fell silent. She smiled. It was the first time they'd met here. She was listening to him talk and was unconsciously playing with the ring; it was too big and she'd dropped it; it rolled under some leaves. They tried to find it, but couldn't and she'd come back the next day to look some more. And here it was; it had surfaced, after all these years. She wiped it on her skirt.

'It's funny that the soldiers didn't find it . . .'

'What soldiers?'

'You know, my darling, the soldiers, the ones who were here during the war, when your papa was wounded.'

'Mama, what's this insect called?'

'It's an ant.'

The little boy stretched out on the ground, his cheek against the earth, watching the insect. Agnès tried to put the ring on, but it didn't fit any more; she'd gained weight since she'd been feeding her daughter. She put down her sewing. She leaned on one elbow. She closed her eyes. Her dishevelled hair was tickling her neck. She was too tired to push it back. Lazy, fleeting thoughts ran through her mind.

It's hot ... I wish we were at the seaside. How annoying that I've made my blouse too tight; I'll have to add an extra panel. 'Guy, you're getting your clothes all green, dragging yourself along the ground like that.' I wonder if Pierre will come and find us? Ah, finally, some air. She sighed, as a puff of wind, a light breeze swept through the pine trees. Maybe there'll be a storm? I want to eat an ice cream, stretched out in the sand, or floating in the sea. 'Guy, don't roll around like that,' she said out loud. 'You'll make yourself even hotter.'

The afternoon passed slowly, with nothing happening. She fed the baby. Guy, who wanted to climb a tree, fell and cut his knee. At three o'clock Madame Florent left; she wanted to stop by the bakery to order some cakes for dinner the next day.

As soon as she had gone Madame Hardelot, now calm (no one could usurp her place in the good graces of little Guy), remembered that she hadn't supervised the ironing of the delicate linen. She hauled herself up, put on her hat over her grey hair and sighed. 'Well, I'm going back, my dear. Don't you rush. It's really hot along the road!'

'We'll be back by six,' said Agnès, knowing that if she got home a few minutes late, she would find Madame Hardelot leaning out of the window, watching the road and exclaiming, 'Finally! I thought you'd died.'

Once her mother-in-law had gone, Agnès tried to pick up her sewing again; it fell from her warm fingers. At four o'clock she took from her bag some jam sandwiches, fruit and biscuits, and poured some cool water into Guy's silver cup. 'Come and eat something, Guy.'

Guy ate his jam sandwich and she watched the wispy clouds around the sun as it began its descent.

'It's impossibly hot, there's bound to be a storm. No doubt the weather will take a turn for the worse when we're at the seaside, it always does. It's funny having found that ring. It's been ten years since I lost it. Only ten years . . . It seems longer. So much has happened . . .'

Absent-mindedly she traced some patterns in the earth with her embroidery needle. 'If, back then, the maid hadn't gossiped . . . If the Hardelot-Arques ladies hadn't seen anything . . . If Saint-Elme hadn't found out that "the Hardelot boy and Mademoiselle Florent were meeting secretly in the Coudre Woods", then I'd be married to someone else now. Happily? Perhaps. How little it takes to turn the course of your life in a different direction.'

She had a sudden thought: 'What is it that binds Pierre and me together so strongly? Why is it that as soon as we got married, we stopped living, suffering, being happy, thinking as individuals? Why have we become so totally one entity? There are couples who never manage it. It's a great mystery and a great blessing.'

'Guy, come here, what are you doing?' she called out. 'Stop throwing those pine cones around; you're going to hurt yourself or your little sister.'

'Mama, can I have your ring?'

'No. What do you want it for?'

'I want to play with it.'

'It's not a toy.'

Once again her thoughts wandered, fleeting and lazy: 'My little girl is growing nicely. She's going to have dark hair. She's going to look like my mother-in-law, unfortunately . . . I heard that Simone Burgères is expecting. She's a guest at the château every Sunday. People must think that idea is tearing me apart. If they only knew . . . But it upsets Pierre. Men are so strange. What time is it? When is Pierre going to get here?'

It was gone five o'clock when she saw him. Whenever she saw him, whether they were alone or in the midst of a crowd, her face, her entire body leaned towards him, as if she were being physically pulled in his direction. And she didn't even realise it.

They didn't kiss. They smiled at each other and he dropped down on to the ground beside her.

'It's so hot.'

'There'll be a storm.'

'My only consolation is the thought of Wimereux. We'll be so happy by the sea ... And all alone. Think of it, Pierre, all alone with our children.'

He looked upset. 'Oh, my poor girl, Wimereux ...'

'What is it?' she asked, worried.

'I don't think we'll be able to go this year.'

'What? Again? This is really too much. Every summer it's the Burgères who get all the holidays and nothing for us.'

'Come on, my darling, you're not being fair. Roland takes his beach walks alone. No chance that his wife will tear herself away from the factory. That woman ... when I think that I nearly married that woman!'

He took her hand. It was so strange; everything brought them closer, even their anger, even the anger they felt towards each other.

Nevertheless, Agnès was furious and she began crushing pine cones between her fingers. 'Your grandfather is an old tyrant,' she said over and over again, 'an old tyrant.'

'You've only just noticed?' he said. 'It's funny. You women are so funny. You endure the worst humiliations with a smile, but when it comes to three miserable weeks ...'

'But those three miserable weeks, alone with you, are my whole life. It's ...'

'Oh, no, please, no scenes, my sweet. It's not like you; you're supposed to be calm, like a cool spring ...'

'No. Don't think you can soften me up with compliments, thank you very much. Do you know what I think? You're a coward. You're getting just like your father. You don't dare open your mouth in front of your grandfather.'

'Listen, Agnès, I knew what to expect when we came back to Saint-Elme. And so did you.'

She wiped away the little tears of rage from the corners of her eyes. 'But why? Did he at least give you a reason?'

'Grandfather never gives reasons, my angel. He just says, "Now . . . Pierre . . . you will stay in Saint-Elme until 1 October. After that, you can go away."'

'But where the hell does he think we can go after the first of October? Where? The Riviera? With small children?'

'I can just picture it,' he said, laughing. 'The Pierre Hardelot family leaving Saint-Elme at the beginning of winter. My mother would have a fit. You know very well that in our family you can only go away between 10 August and 5 September, unless there's a war or mass migration.'

'Even then, it happened at the end of August.'

'You see.'

'No, you're making light of it, but what I'm saying is . . .'

'But what do you want me to do about it?'

They bickered for a few moments. Their little boy ran round them, pretending he was a horse on a merry-go-round and that they were the carousel. They didn't understand his game, so when he tripped over their legs and fell, they shouted, 'Stop that, Guy! You're so annoying. Why are you running round in circles like that?'

'I don't understand,' Agnès finally exclaimed, 'I don't understand how it doesn't upset you. Just think about what our life is like here, between your mother and mine. Never alone, never a moment of freedom, or privacy. But at Wimereux . . . Pierre, we're alone, we're together. We go home. We close our door . . .'

'We do that here too,' he whispered. 'At night, we close our door and we're in our own home. So . . . what more could you ask Agnès?'

They fell silent. A reddish dust, tinged with sap, was rising above the pine trees. The sun was setting.

'Mama, I'm hungry,' said Guy.

Pierre looked at his watch. 'Goodness me! We're late. Hurry up, Agnès. Guy, get your toys together.'

Agnès put the empty bags from their tea, the thermos and the toy horse into the pram. 'It's so annoying,' she thought. 'And it's so hot.'

They left the Coudre Woods and walked along the flat road, burning hot from the sun. They couldn't wait for the cool darkness to come. They brushed aside the day, relegating it to the past, to obscurity, without a single regret. It had been one of the sweetest and most peaceful days of their lives. But they had no way of knowing that.

# 16

It was Julien Hardelot's birthday. He was eighty-five. His family was preparing to celebrate the event in a particularly spectacular way. During the past few months the elderly man had suddenly grown weaker, become hunched with age. Recently he had blacked out briefly, which made the doctor fear that he would soon suffer a stroke. The Hardelots sensed that he wouldn't be with them for long; it was obvious in the way they began talking about him. 'Poor Julien,' they'd say, 'poor grandfather.' He was already benefiting from the kind of sympathy usually reserved for the dead, since the living feel different emotions, more heated and less charitable, towards their peers. When Julien Hardelot got angry, he no longer instilled fear; people just shook their heads. 'Of course, he's not himself any more,' they'd say. His outbursts no longer frightened anyone, but rather evoked a kind of sad pity. They looked at his purplish hands that seemed swollen, stiff, dead. They noticed the hollow sound of his voice. It was difficult to know exactly what the Hardelots were feeling; mostly curiosity, no doubt, about his Will. They thought that Burgères and the young Hardelot would be made partners. They tried to work out what Pierre would get. But everyone agreed that almost the entire fortune of the old man had gradually been sunk into the factory. 'He thought big.' He had taken over rival paper factories; new machinery had been brought over from the United States, at great expense. Roland Burgères had reaped the benefits of that; he'd been able to go to America twice, far away from his wife, all expenses paid.

Finally, in December 1924, they heard that Julien Hardelot was turning his business into a public company. At the news, all of Saint-Elme said the same thing: 'He definitely thinks he's finished. He's doing it to avoid inheritance tax . . .' To the family, another bad sign was his indulgence towards Agnès when it came to his eighty-fifth birthday celebrations. He announced that she would be invited – tolerated – at the dinner that, until now, Pierre had attended alone every year. For all those years, in a desperate, pathetic attempt to save face, Marthe Hardelot had told everyone that Agnès couldn't join the family because she had to stay at home to look after the children. But Guy was eleven now; he would come along with his mother, and Marthe herself would forgo the dinner and stay at home with Colette. No one was taken in. 'He's not the man he used to be,' people kept saying. 'He's gone gaga; now he's making up with Madame Pierre.' This truly seemed proof he was nearing the end. Had the old man softened with age? Was it nothing more than a whim brought on by senility? 'Not at all,' said the two younger Hardelot spinsters (the older two had died at the end of the war of Spanish flu, within a few days of each other), 'not at all. He knows very well that after he dies that young woman will be mistress of his house.'

The women tried to express what, as Hardelots, they vaguely but strongly sensed: that it was far better, far less humiliating to concede a small piece of authority while alive than to see oneself scorned or ignored after death. By receiving Agnès, he seemed to be saying, 'I refused to let you past my front door, but *I* was the one who decided when your punishment would end. So *I* remain in control. No one's going to say that you challenged my authority after my death.'

'And, of course,' thought Agnès, 'he sees the afterlife as a time when his spirit will hover over Saint-Elme and the factory for all eternity.'

She felt anxious about the idea of going to his house. She held Guy's hand tightly in hers; he was wearing long trousers for the first time. He was a thin child, sprightly, with a turned-up nose; his light-blond hair was all tousled at the top of his head like feathers. Ten times a day Agnès smoothed down his wild hair, in vain; it was almost like the silvery down of a little chick. He didn't look like either Agnès or Pierre; the Florent and Hardelot families, despite their best efforts, could not recall a single relative, no matter how distant, who shared any of Guy's features. Pierre and Agnès sometimes joked, 'He must have been switched with another baby in 1914, when everyone was running away.' This was his last year of freedom at home. In September he would be sent away to the boarding school that his father and grandfather had attended.

The young Hardelots waited for the car beneath the glass awning. They only had to go up the road to the château, but Saint-Elme, like all provincial towns, had its own tacit code of behaviour, customs that had to be rigorously followed. No one walked anywhere after dark. And besides, Agnès's satin shoes might have got dirty along the road. It was a winter evening, damp with no wind. The smell of sea fog was in the air, wafting inland from the Channel across the flat countryside. Agnès was wearing a dress of black tulle with the long transparent sleeves in fashion that season.

Even though he wouldn't let it show, Guy was very excited by this invitation. He could sense something strange in the relationship between his mother and his grandfather, but this didn't really surprise him. Vague rivalries divided all of Saint-Elme. Court cases, inheritance issues, old quarrels, political disagreements. These things were taken for granted from childhood, as if they were a necessary counterbalance to the much vaunted familial spirit. As soon as a child was old enough to speak, its ears were filled with whispered warnings during the New Year's Day visits: 'Now, when we're at Aunt Adèle's house, don't mention the electric train that Cousin Jules gave you.' – 'Why not?' – 'Because.' Other things were said in front of the children: 'Why just picture it! I was with Georges when Marie happened to pass by.' – 'What did you do?' – 'Oh, it was embarrassing; they haven't spoken to each other since 1911.'

The war, and especially the years immediately after the war, had made all this bitterness even worse.

The car pulled up. Pierre was driving. None of the families in Saint-Elme had a chauffeur: a car was necessary; a driver was a luxury. The art of living and saving money was summed up in such subtle distinctions.

'This is just like the night when I went to the château in 1914,' Agnès whispered in Pierre's ear.

'They've rebuilt the house exactly like the old one. You'll see. All in all, nothing much has really changed.'

They passed Jault's Inn, the police station and the town hall, whose new stonework shone brightly in the car's headlights. Nothing much *had* really changed, Pierre thought peacefully. He forgot about the terrible injury to his hip that had nearly crippled him for ever, that still caused him so much pain. He forgot that in each of these houses one, two, three men, sometimes more, had not returned.

The car stopped. Agnès got out.

'Be brave,' her husband said, teasing her. He always teased her, she thought tenderly. He went to park the car so she had to go inside alone; Guy had run on ahead with his little cousins.

The elderly man looked shrivelled, shrunken; his cheeks were a deep reddish colour, almost black in places, the colour of dried blood. He held out two fingers to Agnès, without saying a word, and almost immediately turned towards Simone. Every Sunday, at Mass, Simone and Agnès saw each other, said hello and asked after each other's children. But now, beneath the bright lights and without their hats on, they could get a better look at one another. Each woman, a murderous expression in her eyes, noted the defects of her rival in great detail, instinctively homing in on the very feature that time had spared least. For Agnès, it was the fine wrinkles on her forehead and a few grey hairs; for Simone, it was the broken veins on her cheeks and nose, and especially her stoutness that made her look older.

'What a frump,' Agnès thought, but she would have liked to be more beautiful, more elegant herself. 'People age so quickly in the provinces.'

The two women shook hands.

'Isn't Monsieur Burgères here?'

'No. He's gone to Paris for two days. He has to see a client, for your grandfather,' said Simone, knowing full well that Roland had gone to be with his mistress in Paris.

'Oh, really?' said Agnès, who also knew the truth.

The guests were standing around the fireplace, admiring the gift that the factory's workers had given Julien Hardelot that morning. It was a clock of grey marble depicting a stark-naked warrior wearing a Roman helmet, and a scantily clad damsel, her hair crowned with a Phrygian bonnet. These two figures were cast in bronze and their crossed spears rested on the enamel face of the clock whose numbers and hands were gold. The guests looked at the marble and metalwork, trying to assess its value, then respectfully declared, 'It's beautiful. It's heavy.'

Through the darkness you could make out the workers' houses that had sprung up at the foot of the factory and now surrounded the Hardelots' street in every direction. Little lights shone in the windows. They lived right next to each other, but they didn't know each other and didn't like each other. When Agnès had first

94

arrived in Saint-Elme she had wanted to set up a health centre and a day nursery near the factory, but her father-in-law had told her that 'it was pointless', that Julien Hardelot looked after the welfare of his workers himself. Hardelot looked upon everyone born in this place as family. He made sure that the intelligent children were educated and, when they had finished their studies, he gave them jobs. But woe betide anyone who wanted to leave Hardelot's factory! A tacit agreement between the industrialists of the region meant that all doors would be closed to him. Even Hardelot's rivals respected this decree. Hardelot had built inexpensive housing and a school when the workers had asked for them, but refused their request for a swimming pool and a sports stadium. 'The factory is the only place where you need to tire yourselves out,' he'd told them when they'd asked about the stadium; as for the swimming pool, to him it was a pointless luxury. The salaries were low at his factory, but the members of the family (Pierre and the young cousins who also worked for him) were not better treated than anyone else.

'My grandfather's very clever,' Pierre always said. 'He's in charge. He knows that to the ordinary people the misery of everyone is preferable to the happiness of a few. After he has told me off in front of the workers (and Lord knows he can go on!), everything he says to them seems sweetness and light.'

Pierre had just come into the room. He kissed his grandfather and congratulated him; then he went and joined the men standing in front of the fireplace. The ladies were sitting on the settee and the large expanse of the reception room separated the two sexes. The men talked about their cars; it was a topic of conversation they never tired of. They described them lovingly. They passionately compared them to other people's cars. They told gleeful tales of the accidents that had befallen them.

'That hill, you know the one, when you're leaving the village . . .'

'Oh, I know it all right; it's dangerous.'

'It was in 1921 . . . no, January 1922. A truck was parking. There was clearly a red light, but . . .'

The ladies, meanwhile, talked about giving birth. Like soldiers remembering the wounds they suffered at the front, they recalled the event with pride and a shudder. 'With Jean, you know, they had to use forceps . . .' 'Well, when Suzanne was born, *I* . . .' The older ones recounted their stories with a touch of nostalgia. They were like war veterans who say with a sigh, 'When they cut off my leg on the battlefield . . .', implying: 'Those were the days.'

They went in to dinner. All these respectable people leaned over their soup: the men with their heavy, ruddy-cheeked faces, the women, mostly sweet-looking and ageing. The meal was copious and excellent. Old Hardelot looked from left to right along the two rows of guests. He had tucked the corner of his napkin between his chin and his detachable collar. For some time, now, his eyes had been clouded over with a kind of film, like you find in very old dogs. Pierre wondered if his grandfather weren't going blind. But the old man fiercely hid this failing. He wanted to pick up his wine glass; he felt around the tablecloth but couldn't find it.

Pierre pushed the glass towards him. 'Would you like your wine, grandfather?'

He shot Pierre a vicious look. 'No.'

Sometimes he felt an overwhelming drowsiness come over him. In truth, this meal and his family bored him, but it had to be done. All of it was part of what he considered his obligations. Once again, after four years of war, he found himself in a stable world, ruled by unchanging customs and rules. The foundations were solid and wouldn't give way. Everything was in its rightful place. He would leave a universe that had finally been restored to peace and wealth. There had been problems, strikes in Saint-Elme, just like everywhere else. There would be others, the old man thought, but the era of great upheavals was over. And besides, he wasn't overly concerned about the future; for him, the future was particularly restricted. But every now and again a wave of powerful vitality caused him to think, 'I could live to be a hundred.' His own grandfather had died at the age of a hundred and three. He had known him well. But he looked at his purplish stiff hands and shook his head. No. No chance that he would make it to 1942. So what was imperative was that everything remained in good order for another two or three years. And then ... He looked around at his family with the deeply knowing ironic expression common to certain elderly people and certain very ill people, a look that meant 'Soon it will be your turn. Let's see, how do you think *you'll* do?'

Sometimes he forgot the present and drifted back to what remained in his memory of the past, his youth, his parents, whose faces only he now remembered.

Everyone around him could see he was falling into one of those long, deep daydreams from which he would emerge looking lost and confused, as if coming out of a deep sleep.

'He doesn't look well tonight,' they whispered.

After dinner, the young people asked if they could dance. The girls in sky-blue or candy-pink dresses whirled around the room beneath the watchful eye of their mothers, and marriages were arranged. The first shy words were spoken. 'Your Madeleine's nearly eighteen now, isn't she?' Then, 'I wonder whether the son of Achille Renaudin will be back from Paris soon.' Silence, then, 'I always thought he would be suitable for Madeleine ... she's so refined.' — 'I can't get her to stand up straight; it will improve as she gets older,' her mother would say, just as a house owner is quick to mention the minor defects of the property, before the buyer points them out and exaggerates them, touching the wall and saying, 'Look, there's a little scratch

97

here,' imagining it might prevent the buyer from exclaiming, 'But there's a crack.'

'The Renaudin lad is serious and works hard,' someone whispered.

'It would be nice if . . . these children . . .'

And so future events are born out of the darkness.

# 17

'I don't understand this child,' Pierre said to his wife.

It was a September night, warm and ominous; you could smell autumn and a storm brewing, both at once. The Hardelots were sitting in their garden, as they did every evening at this time of year, before going to bed. They'd had to switch off the terrace light because it was attracting the flies. Their white fox terrier lay stretched out at Pierre's feet and their ginger cat was on Agnès's lap. In the house, Colette was playing the piano.

Certain things had changed in Saint-Elme since the night when old Hardelot celebrated his eighty-fifth birthday. He had died a few months later. The factory was now called 'Factory Julien Hardelot – P. Hardelot and R. Burgères: Partners'. The summer of 1933 was drawing to a close. In Europe, it had already been three years since the final gust of victory had drifted away. A gnawing, worrying sense of anxiety gripped everyone. The world resembled a sick man who awakens with a moan, turns over in his bed and tries to forget his troubles, but in vain. Yet on a personal level people's lives were peaceful. They read the papers. They sighed, 'How horrible'. They imagined future wars. They whispered 'America, the Depression, the USSR', then tossed the newspapers to the ground. The maid brought the coffee. A shutter was closed in the sitting room. Agnès looked towards the purple and orange gleam of the patch of zinnias growing beside the lawn, still visible in the growing dark. The stars shone dimly.

'I don't understand this child,' Pierre said again.

It was Guy they were talking about. Colette was still too young. Colette only elicited from Agnès the kind of exclamations that a child of thirteen provokes. 'My God, that girl . . .' she would say quietly, annoyed but affectionate at the same time. Or: 'They're so silly at this age.' Where Guy was concerned it was more serious. He was twenty. Inside the house they could hear his footsteps, sometimes quick and urgent, sometimes slow and weary. This was how the younger generation were, thought Pierre, the generation they no longer understood.

'He never seems to burn with a steady flame,' Pierre thought, reminded, he didn't know why, of the oil lamps he'd seen as a child at his grandfather's house: once lit, their flame would rise, burst upwards, look as if it were about to devour the glass, then, suddenly, it would settle back, grow darker, flicker and almost go out. It took time to adjust it properly, to make sure it was not too strong, not too weak.

'I completely understand that he's bored with us; all children are bored with their parents. I know that in the past, I myself . . .' he said. 'But first of all I didn't let it show,' he continued rather crossly, for the dampness of the evening was causing the old wounds in his arm and hip to hurt.

Agnès broke in. 'I can imagine your father saying to poor Marthe' – she'd died of breast cancer two years earlier and so had earned the title of '*poor* Marthe' or '*poor* darling mother', the epithet reserved for the dead or dying – 'I can imagine your father talking about you, Pierre, saying that he didn't understand you, that the younger generation was unstable, spoiled and immoral.'

'Yes,' Pierre replied quietly. 'They talked about me when they were in bed. Our rooms were right next to each other, and when

Papa got carried away he raised his voice and I could hear him through the wall. I tried to hide under my eiderdown, out of shame, and also because he was making me angry, but I couldn't help hearing what he said about me. And God, he seemed so very . . . naïve. You know, Papa wore those long white nightshirts and they had an enormous bed. A veritable monument. They couldn't get into it without climbing up some steps – they kept them in the alcove; and Mama slept in a night bonnet made of lace, with little purple ribbons, and nightdresses with Valenciennes lace sleeves.'

'I know,' Agnès replied, smiling. 'I make a lot of skirts for Colette out of those nightdresses.'

'Agnès,' Pierre said suddenly, 'Guy must be in love with someone in Paris.'

'But then, why did we let him go there when he was so young . . . ?'

'My dear girl, given his passionate, loving nature, Guy could have met a woman in Saint-Elme, any woman, a worker at the factory, a farm girl or a lady from town, and made the same mistakes as in Paris.'

'But he works so hard at his studies.'

'He works very hard. Better than I did, at his age. I was a plodder, but Guy, Guy is truly gifted.'

He suddenly fell silent.

'He's coming.'

He called out to his son and Agnès made room for him between them on the bench. Pierre offered him a cigarette; he refused absent-mindedly. 'He doesn't smoke. He only drinks water,' thought Pierre. 'He's too good, too good for his age . . . His hands, his eyes, his lips all betray how passionately he feels. It has to be a woman . . . My God, will there never be an end to my problems? You get married, have children, establish yourself, grow old. You think you've managed it all. But no. Everything is just beginning . . .'

His hip was hurting and he let out an annoyed little groan. He was hoping that Guy would say something, the question he himself wouldn't have hesitated to ask if his child had sighed and moaned: 'What's wrong? Don't you feel well?' But Guy said nothing. 'He's egotistical,' Pierre said to himself bitterly, then scolded himself; he was becoming too much like . . . 'a parent'. His son hadn't even heard him groan, the poor child. The confusion in his heart and his senses was undoubtedly so strong that it blocked out anything external, anything that didn't have to do with him . . . and her. Her? But who could she be? In the darkness he tried to make out the face he knew so well, a slim face with a delicate, thin mouth, very pale skin beneath a thick shock of hair. 'Is she a woman who doesn't give a damn about him? Does she want him to marry her? Is there some complication? I must find out,' he thought, feeling repulsed by the idea. Until now, he hadn't been able to make the decision. 'Grandfather and Papa wouldn't have had such scruples. But I'm . . . It's my duty, but . . . And besides, whether she's called Marie or Suzanne, whether she's a blonde or a brunette, what difference does that make to me in the end? There's a woman and she's making him suffer. Those letters he gets . . . and especially the ones he doesn't get, that feigned indifference he assumes every time the post arrives and he asks, "Nothing for me?" And the trips away. Oh, his excuses are always so ingeniously selected. I couldn't have done better myself when I was his age: a friend has invited him to visit, a week in Italy to study a new manufacturing process for making fine paper, sports outings, research . . . and when he comes home: rings under his eyes, absolute silence. Good Lord, it's so obvious. And what's more, Agnès thinks so too,' he told himself, and that fact, in his eyes, was sufficient proof that he wasn't mistaken. Agnès guessed everything and knew everything.

Meanwhile, the silence dragged on and all three of them became embarrassed.

Guy was the first to speak. 'Do you need the car tonight, Papa?'

'No. Why?'

'Because . . . if you wouldn't mind, I'd like to go for a drive to Le Touquet.'

'Now?'

'Yes. It will only take two hours if I drive quickly.'

'And what do you have to do in Le Touquet at this time of night that's so urgent?'

'It's my last week of free time and I'd like to enjoy myself a little; and besides, one of my friends, the Englishman . . . I told you about him, James Robinson, wrote to me to let me know he was spending the weekend in Le Touquet, and I'd really like to . . .'

His father interrupted him abruptly. 'That's enough. Don't bother.'

Guy suddenly leapt up.

Pierre grabbed his sleeve. 'Tell me. What if I said you couldn't take the car?'

'I'd go by bike,' Guy replied quietly.

'And what if I forbid you to go?'

He didn't reply.

'You'd go anyway. Go on then, my boy, go on . . .'

'Guy,' murmured Agnès, a touch of reproach in her voice.

She and Pierre both felt they weren't behaving as they should, that they weren't being firm enough if they really wanted to keep their son from going, nor hypocritical enough if they had really decided to look the other way. My God, how difficult it was to find the right tone, the right balance.

Pierre was tempted to come right out and demand an explanation. He didn't dare. He let his hand fall back. 'Go on then, my boy, go on . . .'

In spite of everything, he couldn't hold back his bitterness. Agnès was wiser; she said nothing, but women are more patient.

'You really seem eager to spend time with us. It's very touching. Thank you so much.'

'But I haven't budged from Saint-Elme in three weeks, Papa. And three weeks in Saint-Elme feels like so much longer. You don't see it, because you've lived here all your life, but I . . .'

'Since you're destined to spend your life here too, you'd do well to get used to it.'

'Well, we'll see about that,' Guy mumbled quietly.

'We'll see? What do you mean?' Agnès exclaimed.

'Oh, don't worry, I'm not about to tell you that I'm leaving Saint-Elme to dedicate my life to literature or to become a Trappist monk,' Guy said, forcing himself to laugh. 'All I'm saying is we'll have to see, because we're certainly headed for another war or revolution, or both. A few years from now there might not be a stone left of your Saint-Elme, nor a single bone or pound of flesh of my body.'

'No! Don't say that,' said Agnès, her voice trembling.

'Be quiet, you fool!' shouted Pierre.

He was ashamed of his angry outburst. Guy, however, replied with extraordinary kindness and a sort of pity. 'Please forgive me; I didn't mean to hurt you. I thought that you could sense, as I do, that everything will inevitably end in a series of violent clashes and that it will be catastrophic, without a doubt. Believe me, there isn't a single twenty-year-old boy who doesn't feel that he is facing a destiny which, at best, could be described as uncertain. And that's really why . . .'

'Why what . . . ?'

'Nothing.'

'Why you want to enjoy fully the time you have left, that's it, isn't it? There's nothing new about that, you know,' Pierre continued, annoyed. 'We felt exactly the same between 1914 and 1918, when we came home from the front.'

'Yes, but you enjoyed yourselves in a base, vulgar way . . . Oh, I don't mean you personally, Papa. I know very well that you were married and a father, it's not you I'm talking about.

I'm talking about your generation, about Burgères, for example. As for me, well, if I'm trying to enjoy life to the full, it's by making life give me its best, its most ideal, its purest, most intense emotions . . . But it's difficult to explain, you wouldn't understand. When you were young, women weren't respected . . .'

'Now we're getting to it,' thought Pierre. He waited.

Guy was aware they were watching him, waiting for him to say something in a moment of weakness. He pulled back.

'But all these generalisations are so meaningless. So listen, Papa, we agree then, you'll give me the car. I hope to be back tomorrow around noon. Unless James Robinson . . .'

'Invites you to stay for dinner and perhaps also to spend the night. In which case you'll phone us and, besides, we have nothing to worry about because James Robinson is very nice, a very serious young man, who has an elderly mother and a younger brother . . . Fine, just fine, as I said, don't bother. It's unbelievable how stupid children think we are.'

'You're being very sarcastic, Papa,' Guy murmured, trying to force a smile.

He stood in front of his parents, head bowed, absent-mindedly digging his heel into the gravel, like when he was a schoolboy, bringing home a bad mark in Latin translation, and the way he resembled a child who has just been scolded touched Pierre, made it impossible for him to torment the boy any longer. Agnès had got up and gone inside.

'And you will do me the favour', grumbled Pierre, 'of not predicting all sorts of disasters in front of your mother. You know that she's had her fair share. You can't remember, you were too young, but when I think of how we had to flee, the destruction of Saint-Elme, those four years of war, my injury . . . Ah, my boy, you might very well say never again, that we'll never see anything like that again, thank goodness, but . . . Go on then, have a good time. Do you . . . do you need any money?'

'Everyone always needs money, but I've just had my allowance and . . .'

'Never mind. Here, take this,' he said, handing him two hundred-franc notes and thinking, 'Maybe if he has this money he won't do anything stupid.' But his indifference towards money proved that the woman in question was wealthy . . .

'And don't drive too fast. It's better if *she* waits for you and sees you arrive in one piece,' he said.

Guy ignored the allusion. He put the money in his pocket, kissed his father and left.

# 18

Pierre was in Paris, trying to get some money.

For three years, now, the machines of Saint-Elme, like those in all the industrial centres of the region, produced expensive merchandise that no one bought. When a supplier finally managed to get some orders, three times out of four the goods were delivered but never paid for: the oldest, most dependable firms were going bankrupt.

'Ours is only still in business thanks to Simone's money. But as for me,' thought Pierre, 'I have none left.'

A third of Julien Hardelot's fortune had disappeared when the Digoin Bank collapsed. It had seemed indestructible, that bank, which for two generations had managed Saint-Elme's money. But it too had died: may it rest in peace. All Pierre's remaining cash had been spent on the factory three years before, but it constantly demanded more investment, a new pot of gold. Every time the money ran out they had to start all over again with new calculations, new loans, new economies, anguishing over how to hold on to their business. Soon Pierre would be forced to hand over his share of the stock to Burgères — he already owed him a large sum — and then it would be goodbye to the factory. He knew that Simone wanted to get rid of him. 'It's because she was in love with you,' Agnès said. 'She's bossy by nature and wants to control you with her money, since she couldn't manage it in other ways when we were young.'

'Just what a woman would think,' he'd reply, but there was some truth in it.

He'd always got along with Roland Burgères. Roland was curiously friendly and respectful towards him; if things had been left to the two of them, it would all have worked out. But Simone! She was fat now, a heavy old woman with hard eyes. She dressed constantly in black, in mourning for her innumerable cousins from the north and the Pas-de-Calais, each of whom died childless and made her their heir. 'Money attracts money,' the Hardelot-Arques and the Hardelot-Demestres said bitterly: they could sense that their reign was at an end, that the sceptre was being handed over. In the sitting rooms of Saint-Elme, the Hardelots were now a diminished lot, a small, frail group of family members, while the ungrateful masses trotted along behind the enormous Madame Burgères (just as they used to follow Julien Hardelot); she walked slowly and, with her ample bosom and vast hips, she seemed to break through the crowd as a frigate breaks through the sea; and behind, in her wake, came her only child, Rose.

'Yes, there might be some truth in it,' thought Pierre when he caught Simone looking a certain way, not at him, never at him, but at Agnès.

He felt the victim of a rivalry between women. 'But if it were only me,' he thought, 'if I were the only one concerned . . .'

What worried him was Guy's future. He could just picture Guy having to beg for work in the factory that had once belonged to his grandfather. When he told Agnès this she was outraged. 'You are joking?' she exclaimed. 'With his intelligence, coming from the best schools, raised the way he has been.'

It was difficult to make Agnès understand that they were living in a world where intelligence, knowledge and education didn't count for much any more: 'Expensive merchandise that no one bought.' No, he had to hold on, at all costs. Besides, that was the only thing you could do, that was the secret to everything, Pierre said to himself.

He felt weary. He had made many calls with no results. These were days when politics outside France seemed dangerous, and politics within the country even worse. Everywhere people looked grave; he overheard desperate talk, full of strange, mournful despair, as if the world was accepting its death sentence without a single word, without rebelling, with just a low, weak whimper. He had asked his usual bankers for unsecured loans, in vain; he had then offered the deeds to his house as collateral. Nothing worked. The wisest thing would be to go directly to Roland. Simone held the purse strings, but Roland had his own personal line of credit, especially since the doctors had discovered that Simone had a heart defect . . . Pierre suddenly remembered, in extraordinary detail, those evenings on the beach at Wimereux in 1910, his engagement to Simone. He recalled the engagement dinner and everything that had followed, and he felt a bitter, profound sense of melancholy, like the taste that stays in your mouth after you drink cheap wine. Everything around him was grey and sad. He walked across the Champs-de-Mars: he was going back to Guy's place. It was a May evening, but freezing cold, with a fine mist that turned into rain, as in deepest autumn. He passed some young people coming home from school, briefcases full of books under their arms; they ran to catch the AX bus and Pierre could hear their laughter.

'To think that they might remember the spring of 1936 as a sweet, happy time,' thought Pierre. 'There are satisfied lovers, joyful children all around me today, but to me, everything seems gloomy. Ah, it's because I don't like being away from Agnès and Colette. I've become such a stay-at-home, my God, poor, good bourgeois that I am . . . I sink back into my shell and forget the world. But the world won't let you forget, the rotter. Now what?

Go and see Roland? Appeal to his sense of honour, to our friendship? Ask him to intervene with Simone, so they give me an
extension, so they pay the Baumberger bill? Stall for time, hold
on . . . until the next disaster? Bah! You do what you can each
day. I'm not going to imitate the Jeremiahs who cover their heads
in ashes. Things will work out because everything in life ends up
in a kind of modus vivendi, a way of dealing with misfortune,
which is all that anyone can reasonably hope for. I must discuss
it with Guy, he thought. He's old enough to give his opinion.
He knows Burgères well; they're friends. I even think it was
Burgères who introduced him to this woman . . .'

He frowned; any reminder of Guy's love affair, still as mysterious, still as secretive, still as passionate as it was three years ago,
upset and annoyed him. He walked more quickly to his son's place.
He was eager to see him. How long it all took – his apprentice-
ship, his education, his military service. He wished that Guy could
come back home.

He sighed. He crossed the exhibition space that separated the
Champs-de-Mars and the Esplanade. Suddenly, in the darkness of
the night, fireworks shot out of the top of the Eiffel Tower: they
were testing them before the beginning of the holidays. Their
flames and sparks seemed strange and mournful as they fell down
on to the deserted, damp gardens. The rain was falling, and through
it you could hear the explosions and the long whistle the fireworks
made as they faded away. Finally, Pierre could see the building
where his son lived. He quickly closed his wet umbrella and went
upstairs.

Guy was subletting the flat from one of his cousins, an officer
in Morocco. Pierre and Agnès were happy to spare their son the
experience of living in a sordid hotel in the Latin Quarter, but
sometimes Pierre thought he might have given Guy his freedom as
a man too soon. He recalled his own student days: 'Even a woman
in love would have thought twice about setting foot in the Hôtel

des Grands-Hommes, where the frugalness of the Hardelot family shut me away when I was twenty,' he mused. Guy, on the other hand, could afford the most elegant of mistresses. This mysterious affair was still going on, he was sure of it. 'But the boy will nevertheless have to go back to Saint-Elme, and then . . . Unless, in the meantime . . .' He sighed. Nothing was certain, that was the hardest thing. 'A Hardelot needs to know exactly where he stands, even if it is right in the middle of hell. After all, I lived in hell for four years. But Lord, at least I knew where I was, whereas now, it's this sort of limbo, this fog, this mirage. That's what is unbearable. Bah! Everyone suffers from it these days, this great, vague anxiety, and the history books are bound to say: "Between 1920 and 19**, the world experienced a period of relative contentment . . ." Of course, but Guy hasn't reached that point yet,' he murmured, ringing the bell for the second time. No one was answering.

'What's going on? I'm sure we were meant to have dinner together tonight, 8 May!'

He rang again. Finally he heard footsteps and Guy opened the door. His shirt had no collar and he hadn't shaved. He looked at his father for a moment as if he didn't recognise him.

'Are you ill?' Pierre asked anxiously.

'Yes . . . I feel rotten, I'm coming down with something; I was sleeping . . . I'm sorry, Papa, come in, quickly.'

'But what's wrong with you? Did you call the doctor?'

'Don't be ridiculous, come on. It's just a touch of flu, I'm sure. You know, with the weather we're having . . .'

'Do you have a fever?'

'Definitely not.'

Pierre felt his forehead. 'No, you feel cool. But you look so . . .'

'But I'm telling you, Papa, it doesn't matter.'

'Fine. Don't get angry,' Pierre said sadly, realising he was upsetting him. 'But listen, son, I've come over for dinner. If you only have aspirin to offer me . . .'

'No, don't worry. The concierge is coming up with a good meal for us in a few minutes.'

He had led Pierre into the dining room, where two places had in fact been laid at the table. They both sat in silence, looking at each other and feeling very distant from one another. Finally, Guy asked for news of the family. While Pierre was answering, he interrupted with a sudden urgent, almost brutal, gesture: 'Wasn't that the phone?'

'No.'

Nevertheless, Guy grabbed the receiver and shouted 'Hello, hello' several times, in vain. Pierre had turned away.

'You were right,' Guy finally said, sounding crushed. 'I took a bit of quinine and I can hear buzzing in my ears. You were saying that Mama ...'

They continued their conversation in a cold, restrained manner. They were both tormented by anxiety and spoke familiar words almost haphazardly: 'Your mother' ... 'Your work at the factory ...' These words led to other, similar ones, without either father or son needing to think. Pierre took off the glasses he had started to wear, for his eyes were getting worse; he studied their horn-rimmed frames with a sad, absorbed expression, blew gently on the lenses, cleaned them and stared vaguely into space. For a while, now, his mannerisms had become similar to those of his dead father Charles; he was aware of it. It annoyed him, but there was nothing he could do about it. More than ever, he was now determined to tell Guy about all his financial problems. 'A new problem takes your mind off the old one,' thought Pierre. But he didn't know how to tell him the truth. Every way seemed dangerous, complicated: 'And what if he reproaches me for having managed our affairs badly? No, he's a respectful boy. But what if he thinks it? ... Oh, that would be unfair, hurtful ... And if he's on the verge of doing something stupid, getting married or ... Will it hold him back or have the opposite effect?'

He was so upset that he had stood up and was pacing back and forth in the room. Both of them were silent now. Guy had sunk back into a chair and was slowly, nervously, tearing up a book that he had open on his lap.

'What on earth are you doing?' his father finally asked.

The young man started. 'Me? Nothing.' He leapt up. 'I'll go and see what's keeping our dinner.'

Pierre remained alone for rather a long time. He absent-mindedly rearranged the cushions on the settee. A small gold compact containing some powder and a puff fell on to the carpet. Forcing himself to laugh, Pierre handed it to his son as he came into the room: 'Here, this must belong to one of your teachers.'

Guy frowned, took the compact and put it in his pocket without saying a word. The bell rang. Guy went pale, started walking towards the door, then stopped and murmured, 'I'm so stupid. It's just the concierge.'

It was indeed her; she came in, apologising for being late. If the gentlemen would like to sit down at the table, the soup was ready. She served it and the two silent men, sitting opposite each other, swallowed a few spoonfuls. The concierge came back, looked at the bowls, still half full, and asked in a rather dejected tone if 'the soup was not to their liking'. Guy didn't reply and Pierre mumbled that it was excellent but that he wasn't hungry. The ham omelette and cold veal arrived at the same time, then the concierge set out plates of fruit and cheese, told them the coffee was on the stove and left. When he heard her heavy footsteps going down the back stairs, Pierre thought: 'Now's the time . . .'

'Listen, my boy,' he began.

He spared him nothing. He explained in detail the collapse of the Digoin Bank, his growing financial difficulties, his vain attempts, that very day, to get hold of some money. He wanted to make an impression on Guy, frighten him; anything was better than the morose indifference with which his son listened to him. Finally, Pierre could stand it no longer. 'Well, what do you think about it all, eh?' he asked.

'Nothing,' Guy replied.

'Meaning?'

'Nothing. It doesn't really surprise me. It's the same every-where.'

'But you at least have some ideas, don't you?'

'About what?'

'About the future. About your future.'

'I don't see my future as separate from yours,' said Guy more gently, 'but, my poor Papa, there's nothing to be done but to brace yourself against the storm and wait. Either things will work out, or everything will break down. It's not your work, nor the Hardelot companies that are the issue, but a vast, complex machine of which you, we, are only a tiny cog.'

When Pierre mentioned Burgères, he suddenly became agitated. 'Oh, no! Don't ask Burgères for anything, not him. Nothing, I'm begging you! I can't stand him.'

'Really?' replied Pierre, surprised, 'I thought you were friends.'

Guy pushed away his plate. 'No. What a thought! No! We are not friends. We have a few friends in common and that's all. Papa, be careful of Burgères. You can't count on him.'

'You're wrong.'

'Oh, so that's what you think?'

'Listen, I wouldn't trust him with a woman, but, apart from that . . .'

'Ah,' murmured Guy.

He fell silent, then asked with pained annoyance, 'But really, what do women see in him? To start with, he's old.'

'Oh, Guy, don't be so unkind; he's younger than me.'

'Yes . . . well, but I'm being serious, Papa. Do you think he's attractive, well, do you?'

'I don't know, my boy, I never thought of him that way: I'm not interested in what he looks like. Are you jealous of him?'

Guy's face went completely white. 'Don't be ridiculous,' he said.

'But you're asking ridiculous questions. I'm talking to you about Burgères and the factory and you ask me if I find him attractive. Come on, get a grip on yourself, my boy. These are serious matters. I was thinking of asking Burgères if I could go and see him tonight.'

'Tonight? You mean he's here in Paris?'

'Yes. For a few days. And, my word, away from that damned Simone it will be easier . . . But what's the matter? Aren't you listening? Are you ill?'

'No, I . . . Oh, but that's the telephone, I'm positive this time,' Guy exclaimed, extraordinarily elated, and he ran to pick up the receiver.

'Hello, hello, I'm here!' he said in a frenzy.

Then he lowered his voice and turned towards Pierre.

'It's for you, Papa, it's a call from Saint-Elme.'

It was Agnès. 'Don't worry,' she said, 'everything's all right at home. But something terrible has happened to Burgères.'

'To Burgères?' murmured Pierre. 'We were just talking about him. Hello, can you hear me?' he shouted.

'We just got a call from Versailles. There was a car accident on the road between Saint-Cyr and La Trappe. He's dead, the poor thing. Simone and Rose are leaving for Paris, but they've asked if you would please go to Versailles right away to take care of the formalities, if possible. Is Guy all right? Send him my love, and love to you as well, my darling . . .'

He could hear Agnès kissing the phone. He said goodnight to her and walked back over to Guy. 'Well, there it is . . . Poor man . . . poor bloke . . . He was always nice to me and he fought bravely in the war. You won't have anything more to complain about where he's concerned. Well, goodbye. I have to go to Versailles. How awful . . .'

'I'm going with you.'

'You're not well, my boy. I don't need you to come.'

'I'm going with you,' Guy repeated. Then, after a moment's silence, he asked, 'How exactly did he die?' His voice sounded strange.

'I told you: in a car accident.'

'Was he alone?'

'We'll find out in Versailles,' Pierre replied curtly.

Neither of them spoke on the way there. Guy had taken the compact out of his pocket and was gently stroking it. Once at the hospital, his father told him to wait in the reception area. He obediently sat down by a window and watched the rain fall beneath the street lamp.

Finally, Pierre came back. 'He was still alive when they found him on the road. He died on the way to the hospital. I don't think he suffered.'

'Papa, was he alone?'

'Yes,' said Pierre.

'Are you telling me the truth?'

'Yes.'

'Do you swear?' Guy insisted.

'I swear,' Pierre replied, hesitating for an instant. He took his son by the arm. 'Let's go now.'

Guy gently pulled away. 'Wait, I want to see him.'

'But why?'

'Because. After all, Papa, you were right before: we were good friends and I want to say goodbye to him. Wait for me here, Papa.'

'All right, then, go on,' Pierre replied, reassuring himself that the nurses had been given strict instructions and his son would never find out there had been a woman in the car with Burgères. The woman hadn't been hurt and had gone home. It might have been better for Guy if . . . He shook his head.

Guy, meanwhile, had gone into the little room where Burgères's body was laid out. For a long time he studied the tall, handsome body, the battered face. The dead man had been undressed and he lay there, covered by a sheet. His bloodstained clothes had been placed on a chair.

'I'd like to be alone with him for a minute,' Guy said to one of the nurses. 'He was a friend of mine.'

As soon as she went out he grabbed Burgères's jacket and waistcoat, rushed over to the light, pulled out his wallet, opened it, leafed through the letters inside, trembling with fear and disgust. Nothing, he found nothing.

He called the nurse back inside. 'There's a thousand francs for you,' he said, showing her the money, 'a thousand francs if you tell me who was with this man when he died. His wife will be here soon. She mustn't know anything. But you can tell me.'

She hesitated for a moment. 'There was a woman with him,' she said finally.

'Blonde, slim, very bright eyes, wearing a red necklace, dark garnets in the shape of stars?'

She nodded 'yes'.

'Was she wearing a white straw hat with a red ribbon?' he persisted, 'or a grey felt hat, or . . .'

'A dark-red felt hat with a black ribbon.'

'Ah, her dark-red felt hat,' he murmured. 'And, Mademoiselle, are you sure, very sure about the necklace?'

She looked at the money. 'Very sure,' she said.

'Was she hurt?' Guy asked quietly.

'No, not a scratch.'

Guy picked up his hat, glanced one last time at Burgères's body and went out to Pierre.

'You were in there a long time,' said his father.

Guy said nothing. They left, in silence.

# 19

Burgères's body was transported to Saint-Elme and buried beneath the memorial built for Simone's parents; on it was a carved figure with a long beard, kneeling on a stone cushion, wearing a cloak that fluttered in the wind, while an angel touched his shoulder with one hand; the angel's other hand pointed towards the factory chimney, visible above the cypress trees. Guy walked behind the coffin with all the Hardelots and Renaudins, threw some holy water into the open grave, bowed to Simone and Rose, went back home, had lunch, did, in a word, everything he should have done, everything that was expected. Then he said goodbye to his family, went back to Paris and, that same night, shot himself twice in the chest.

Pierre had slept badly, haunted by sinister dreams; he was resting after lunch. He was awakened by the sound of the telephone and Agnès screaming as she came and threw herself down on the bed, sobbing.

They left for Paris together. They were told that Guy was dying. He could go at any moment. When at last they arrived at the hospital, after a journey that felt like an incoherent nightmare, they were told that the surgeon was operating on Guy, that they were doing everything and more to save him. They were asked to wait. They waited, sitting side by side on the green velvet settee,

in the sad room reserved for visitors. They were not alone. Other
people were waiting like them. No one said a word. A muffled
sigh sometimes escaped from a heavy heart and when the door
opened, all the pale, pained faces looked up at the nurse as she
came in. All their lips moved softly, silently. All their trembling
hands clasped each other, clutched on to one another or clung
nervously on to the arm of the chair. At that time of night they
only operated on the most urgent cases, people who were extremely
ill. But the nurse walked through the room and noticed nothing
but her face in the mirror. She was young and pretty; she adjusted
her hat, went out. The door closed behind her.

Pierre and Agnès didn't have the courage to speak to each other,
or look at each other, or hold each other's hand. The pain they
felt was like none they had ever felt before; it didn't bring them
closer; it was too different in each of them. Agnès's pain was
violent and overwhelming, devoid of thought or will, nothing but
the physical pain she had felt when she'd given birth to this child.
Pierre's pain was thoughtful and bitter. His son, his Guy, to be
capable of this, this sin, this cowardice! He didn't dare turn to
look at Agnès. What could he possibly say to her? Their burning
hands had touched for just a second. Absent-mindedly he pushed
back a lock of grey hair that had come loose from under Agnès's
hat and silently she pushed him away. She didn't see him any
more, didn't recognise him any more. She wanted her son. He
was finally returned to her, after that long night. He was alive.
'He has a chance,' she was told. He didn't say a word. He accepted
her care and attention with the same indifference he accorded the
nurse. Sometimes it even seemed to the despairing Agnès that he
preferred the nurse, a stranger, whose reproach he didn't fear.

They remained in Paris all spring. They stayed at a hotel near
the hospital. They only lived now for the few hours each day
when they were allowed into Guy's room, when they sat, in silence,
one on each side of his bed, when they listened to him groan,

when they watched over him, when they waited for the doctor to visit, when they stared at the white chart that kept track of his fever.

They had aged a lot in those few weeks. Their faces were thin, ravaged, and their eyes surrounded by dark rings. During moments of half-consciousness that followed nights of delirium, Guy wondered why they had changed so much. Then he would forget them. He thought about the woman who had cheated on him with Burgères. He thought about his own life. His father and mother were so distant to him, so good, he mused, so detached, so calm. They were how you imagine the dead: in a pure, warm place, while on earth you burn and devour your own heart. Agnès's hand stroked his forehead, held his hand; he fell asleep.

One day he was stretched out like this, without moving. But he was feeling better. The doctor spoke words of hope. The strange coldness between Pierre and Agnès melted. Quietly, for the first time, their voices faltering, they spoke of things they had never thought about, of their youth, of love, of passion, of the madness that had driven their child to suicide.

'But didn't you ever find out the name of the woman?'

'No,' replied Pierre, 'what good would it do?'

'But if he recovers he'll want to see her again.'

'But she won't want to see him. She hasn't even been to see him once, has she? She hasn't tried to find out how he is, I know that for a fact. It was an affair that lasted three years and she got tired of him, that's all there is to it.'

They fell silent.

'I don't understand this child,' Pierre whispered again, sadly.

They began to talk about themselves, their past.

'Would *you* have been able to do this?'

'No. I feared God. What about you?'

He didn't reply.

'But you were never jealous,' said Agnès with a faint smile. Her features lit up with that fleeting brilliance of youth that adorns the faces of wise, mature women when they speak of love.

'I was jealous,' said Pierre, 'when we were young and I found out you were engaged to Lumbres, and I imagined his butcher's hands on your body . . . and, during the war, I felt the worst kind of jealousy, for no reason, the kind that is born out of an idea, a sigh, a dream. I trusted you, I respected you, but I knew what a mad time we were living through and what some women did while we were away . . .'

'Well, *I* was jealous of Simone and even now, when I see her, I feel . . .'

She broke off. She placed her hands on her throat.

'I've never loved anyone but you,' said Pierre, without looking at her.

'I know,' she replied softly. 'I know everything about you. When you were attracted to another woman . . . don't deny it, it's happened to you just as to everyone. Even before you were touched by desire, I was already being tortured by it. But I know you've never loved anyone but me.'

He took her hand. 'My poor wife,' he said shyly, and he smiled, because he was using the same words that Charles used to Marthe in the past.

They fell silent, both of them smoothing their son's bed, and such warmth and tenderness flowed from them that they were a little ashamed to be so old and still so in love.

'He's going to get better,' thought Agnès, looking at Guy's face. 'Things will soon be as they have always been.'

They felt as if they had gone through the worst trial of their lives, that finally it was all over, that all they had to do now was to make their way along life's straight and easy path, two old horses, harnessed together, bearing the same burden, until they died.

Guy woke up and asked for something to drink.

# 20

Simone paid the bills due on 31 May and 30 June. Towards mid-
July 1936, Pierre, who was still in Paris with the convalescing Guy,
received a note from Simone asking him please to come to Saint-
Elme, even for only forty-eight hours, 'to sort out some urgent
matters'. He read her letter with a heavy heart. During Guy's
illness his financial problems had seemed of no importance whatsoever. His boy had to get well; nothing else mattered. Now that
his son was recovering, his problems at the factory became his
main concern once more. They disturbed the little bit of sleep he
still managed to get. He found it horrible to talk to Simone about
money, to stand in front of a woman like a beggar. While Burgères
had been alive, Simone never openly intervened between her
husband and her ex-fiancé, even though she controlled everything.
What's more, she was one of those women who only ever says
things like 'My husband would prefer it if . . . It's what my husband
wants . . . My husband has expressly forbidden me to do that . . .'
Rich as she was, and even though she'd learned how to protect
her fortune to such an extent that Burgères had been forced to go
to moneylenders more than once, if she cancelled an order for a
hat from her milliner, she would add, 'My husband thinks it's too
expensive.' This was a way of thinking she had inherited, combined

with a sense of propriety. A woman should never be forward. She had raised Rose according to these principles. But Rose was haughty and intelligent; she had Burgères's temperament and clashed with her mother on this subject, as well as on many others.

When old Hardelot had died, Pierre and Agnès had refused to live in the château, so the Burgères had bought it. Even though Pierre told himself, often and out loud, that he hated the oppressive building and was happy he didn't live in it, every time he crossed its threshold he felt dispossessed. Today more than ever. He walked up the path along which, in the past, Julien Hardelot would take his evening walks in the summer, passed the garage wall, all that remained of the original house, its stones still bearing traces of the flames that had scorched it. He went into the reception room with its closed shutters, its covered furniture. The room smelled of polish and camphor, just as it had in his grandfather's day. The chandeliers were carefully wrapped in brown paper and yellow gauze. Only the piano was partially uncovered: someone had forgotten to close it and put back its dust cover. Simone came in and, seeing the piano, frowned, apologised, went to the door and called out, 'Rose!'

The young girl came in (she was only sixteen, but strong and shapely, with brown hair, lustrous skin and thick, dark eyebrows) and said hello to Pierre.

'Rose,' was all her mother said, pointing at the keyboard.

Without replying, Rose slammed the lid shut with such force that the chandelier tinkled, despite being doubly wrapped. Pierre hadn't seen the girl for more than two years, for she was at boarding school in Belgium, and during the holidays her mother travelled with her to England and Austria, to help her improve her languages: Simone was the perfect mother. Pierre thought back to the silent, docile little girl she used to be. She had certainly changed. The constant battle between the two women was obvious in the haughty looks Simone flashed and the silent rage on Rose's face.

She started to walk away. 'Rose,' her mother said again.

She hadn't replaced the cover. The young girl came back, leaned over, set it in place and left without a word, but with a final furious look at her mother.

Simone picked up her black-edged handkerchief from the table and began fanning herself. She wore, of course, the heaviest mourning clothes and even though it was difficult to make distinctions in such things, Pierre thought he had never seen such a deep, harsh shade of black as the one she wore. From her collar to the tips of her toes, she was all black crêpe and jet necklaces. On the mantelpiece stood a portrait of Roland Burgères, painted at his deathbed.

'She has a very difficult nature,' said Simone, raising her eyes to heaven as soon as Rose had gone. 'But I don't have to tell you, my dear friend, what problems our children cause us ... How is your poor boy?'

'Fine,' Pierre replied curtly. 'Thank you for asking.'

He found it repulsive that she should talk to him about Guy, that she should judge Guy. Did she know how her husband had died? He held her responsible for the attempted suicide. He knew it was unfair, but still ... 'This woman has always brought me misery,' he thought. 'Everything that happens to me because of her is bad. Because of her, Agnès was rejected by my family. Because of her husband, my child has suffered. She stripped me of my fortune ...'

Out loud he said, 'Is there something you need to tell me?'

'Yes. I understand nothing about business, as you know. My poor husband took care of everything. But now that he is no longer with us I am forced to do my best as far as running the factory is concerned. You know, don't you, that I paid the last two months' bills?'

'I am very grateful to you.'

She waved her fat hand. 'Of course. You are going through

such difficult times. I am a mother, I understand. I have barely
had time to mourn my poor husband myself. I've been plagued
by a mountain of problems, both mine and yours. I personally
took care of Baumberger's bill; that brings our accounts to . . .'

She broke off.

'They worked out the account this morning at the office. Please
forgive me for being obliged to look through the paperwork. I've
never had a head for numbers,' she continued, opening her handbag;
it was black, with an ebony frame, dark, heavy and solid, like her.

Pierre stretched out his hand and stopped her. 'Dear friend, I
know the figures by heart and they are (need I say, since you
know it as well as I do) well beyond my current means. I hope
you don't wish to ruin me? Are you demanding that I pay you
what I owe you at once?'

Like all women, a direct question unnerved her. Her haughty,
sullen face blushed slightly. 'Please know, my dear Pierre, that
only the most pressing necessity is forcing me to speak to you like
this. The situation in which I find myself is difficult. I have an
enormous number of financial matters to deal with. I'm not used
to running a business . . .'

'Oh,' murmured Pierre.

Each of us remains faithful to the idea we have of our true
nature, our spirit and our character. Simone obviously clung fast
to her role as a weak, gentle woman, submissive before masculine superiority. It was a role, thought Pierre, that had been instilled
in her since childhood. She had performed it at her very best when
they were young, when she took pride of place on the sandy beach
at Wimereux-Plage, as the chaste fiancée, in a pink dress, the
ribbons of her waistband fluttering behind her. Without a doubt,
in her own eyes she hadn't changed. She lowered her heavy, wilting
eyelids, with an air of innocence.

'I would love to be able to live like Agnès, quietly in my corner,
I can assure you . . . Unfortunately, that's impossible. You knew

Roland. The poor man had a generous, impulsive nature. He has left a lot of debts, a very complicated situation, very sensitive. The company is in grave danger, make no mistake, Pierre. We have done our best, but everything is working against us: taxes, social policies, the wholesale price of materials, the economic crisis, which looks endless.'

'I know all this as well as you, dear friend,' Pierre said coldly.

'But while you've been away, the situation had grown worse. You have no idea how many nights I've spent trying to find a way, calculating, working things out. At the moment we have one order from England, but after that, if we don't get some more money to invest in the factory, we're finished, finished. We'll have to file for bankruptcy. The Hardelot and Burgères factory going bankrupt, the workers out on the street . . . think of your poor grandfather. We owe it to his memory to preserve the business he founded. Personally, I can tell you that I've sacrificed everything. And I'm not even counting all the loans made against my dowry. But now I have my daughter's future to protect. I see only one solution: I'll have to pull out of the business, if I can, and go and live in peace in the Midi, with Rose, far from Saint-Elme.'

Pierre said nothing. He knew that if she even hinted in Saint-Elme that she intended to pull out of the factory he'd be finished. All the existing credit would be cut off. She would ruin him, because in order to avoid bankruptcy he would spend every penny he had, all of Agnès's savings; he was a Hardelot; he would not be disgraced. But if he sold his shares to Simone, he thought, the factory would be saved.

'Your grandfather left you with a heavy burden,' she said. 'He was very rich, but for a fortune to last from generation to generation it needs constant reinvestment, sustained by inheritances . . .'

'Or by marriages,' said Pierre.

He could barely conceal his anger. He looked at her with hatred.

Agnès was right. Simone still held their broken engagement against him, after twenty-six years. These women, good Lord, these women . . . It was only by thinking of Agnès, by picturing Agnès's sweet face that he finally calmed down.

'What are you proposing?' he asked.

She hesitated.

'It would be possible to help you this time, once again . . . oh, not you, but the company. It's only the company that's the issue, you know that very well. It's clear that we are both prepared to make sacrifices so the company can survive. What I could do would be to sell my mother's jewellery; Rose will reproach me for it one day, but too bad. With that money I could buy out your shares and then you would owe me nothing.'

'The shares are worth more than that, as you know very well.'

'And you know what you were offered for them in Paris,' she said, turning away so he couldn't see the look of triumph on her face. She had made sure she was well informed.

After a moment she leaned towards him. 'You can't have everything,' she said quietly. 'You're happy with Agnès and your delightful children. Your family can be your consolation for your difficulties.'

'Don't bring my family into this.'

'Why not? It affects them. Do you think that Agnès will reproach you for having regained your freedom? All in all, this factory is a burden. You'll have enough money to live on. And you're not like your grandfather who cared about nothing in the world except the factory. It was his passion; it isn't yours. I envy you. A business like this is less certain, more dangerous than a love affair. Think of the cost of running it, of working in it, of worrying about it and what it will cost in future . . . And think of how many people would love to get their hands on it. How vulnerable it is,' she insisted. 'After me, Rose will inherit it. So her husband will become the head of it. What kind of husband? Sometimes I can't sleep for worrying about that. She's not the kind of girl you can marry off as you please; she's so stubborn. But I've become attached to the factory. I was brought up with the idea that one day it would belong to me and it must have been in my blood, you understand, because even though I gave up the man, I couldn't give up the company. And since then I've grown even more strongly attached to it. People become attached to other people or to bricks and mortar; I don't know which is wiser. Here is a company that should be the best in the country but is on the verge of bankruptcy. Why? If there were a reason, at least, or if it were my own fault. But no . . . Sometimes everything is handed to you, sometimes it is all taken away and you never know why. So I will save the business this time. Agreed? But then what? . . . Do I know what laws they'll come up with next? Do I know whether war will break out tomorrow? Or revolution? Or . . . In such circumstances I will have sacrificed my youth, my happiness, for nothing. Roland hated Saint-Elme. He was . . . I don't want to talk about it: he's dead. I don't get along with Rose. She knows that all the money belongs to me and that she can't do as she pleases. I'm telling you all this . . . because we've known each other such a long time and we've never spoken honestly to each other. This is all I have left,' she said, pointing to the chimneys of the factory.

Pierre too looked out at them with a strange feeling that was a mixture of bitterness and pity. The Hardelots had lived for this factory. They had married ugly women; they had skimped and counted every last penny; they had been rich and had enjoyed fewer pleasures than the poor. They had stifled their children's interests, thwarted their loves. All this for the factory, for their possessions, for something that was, to their eyes, more durable and faithful than love, women or their own children. When Julien Hardelot thought Charles was a fool, he comforted himself by thinking that the factory, at least, was a product of his very own inspiration and wouldn't let him down. When his wife had died, he had stood and contemplated the bricks and the land that comprised his business, and peace had returned to his heart: everything else was ephemeral, but his possessions would endure. Pierre himself had shared this illusion. Was it an illusion or reality? He didn't know, couldn't know. No one knew. It was one of God's secrets. But at the moment, property was almost as much at risk as human life. Simone was right. To him, at least, the factory was gone for ever.

He pulled himself out of his reverie and turned towards Simone with a sigh. He would leave Saint-Elme, go and live in Paris. He wouldn't be bored. He would take Agnès to concerts, the theatre. He would read all the history books that interested him and that he'd never had the time to take notes on, to study, as he had wanted to. He would grow old in peace. He would have more friends in Paris than in this provincial place where, even to this day, Agnès was considered an intruder and treated with cold contempt. Adieu, Saint-Elme!

# 21

On the eve of 1 January 1938, Pierre Hardelot and his wife were alone in Paris, in their little apartment on the Boulevard de Courcelles. Colette, who had passed her exams in October and was now studying Law at the university, had been invited to a party; she had gone out an hour earlier, very happy, in a new dress. The previous night Guy had said that he would stay in, that he'd go to bed early, but ageing parents who are still in love create an atmosphere of ghost-filled, contented melancholy that is intolerable to the young. So, having drunk a glass of champagne with them, Guy had ended up going out for the rest of the evening. He had found a position as an engineer in a factory; he led an ordered, gloomy life, as if, two years ago, he had spent all the passion, all the pain, all the love of which he was capable. With his parents he was more affectionate than before, but even more distant. What he read, his friends, his thoughts were unknown to Pierre.

So the husband and wife were alone. Pierre opened another bottle of champagne. The year 1938 began cold; light snow was falling. They lit the fire in the dining room. The radio was on low in the darkness. Pierre was assessing the year that had just passed.

'What will *this* year bring?' he asked. 'We looked forward to the past two years with such confidence (like this one too, alas, like this one too), but they had nothing much to offer: that business with Guy . . .'

'Oh, please don't talk about it,' murmured Agnès.

'Poor Roland's death, our problems, the money we lost, the factory taken over by someone else. I wonder what this year will bring?' he said again.

'Well, you've already had your first gift . . .' said Agnès, touching her husband's hand, '. . . a bad cold. Please, go to bed and don't drink any more cold champagne.'

'It does me good,' said Pierre, coughing.

The next day he had a fever. Half of Paris was ill that winter; he had flu, complicated by a chest infection, which kept him in bed for two weeks. Meanwhile the last of the Hardelot-Arques ladies died, making Pierre her heir. But all she had was a few pieces of silverware and some furniture she'd bought in the Faubourg Saint-Antoine during the Great Exhibition of 1900. It had been badly damaged by having sat in the basement for four years during the war, so it was immediately obvious that this inheritance would bring nothing but problems with the taxman. Neither Pierre nor Agnès could travel to Saint-Elme to attend the elderly lady's funeral and deal with her affairs, so Guy had to go. He received permission to be away from work for three weeks (which would be deducted from his annual holiday). He would stay with his maternal grandmother, Madame Florent, who had never left Saint-Elme, despite her hatred for the sleepy, cold little town. How she had dreamed of getting away from it. But when it had been possible, when Agnès had offered her a room in their Parisian apartment, it was too late. She had reached the age where you recoil at the idea of any kind of change, as if it were an omen of the greatest change of all: death. Like all the good middle-class ladies of Saint-Elme, she barely left her house; she fell asleep reading the papers; she got a new maid every six months. This was her only entertainment now. It excited her, annoyed her, added a little spice to her life. She had no money left whatsoever: her husband's legacy had been spent on Agnès's Russian bonds. Her children sent her money every month. She was very happy to see her grandson; she gave him the bedroom next door to hers and, at every meal, made him all the dishes he had liked as a child but which now, sadly, were the ones he most disliked as an adult.

The elderly Mademoiselle Hardelot-Arques was buried. All of Saint-Elme was present in the new little church. The black curtains at the entrance fluttered in the soft wind that blew in from the sea on rainy days. During Mass, the clouds in the sky vanished; a silvery ray of sunlight lit up the white flagstones, the blue statue of the Virgin Mary and the one of Joan of Arc, whose tunic was painted blue and gold. The candles around the bier were reduced to transparent flickering flames and from the coffin rose columns of luminous dust that floated upwards towards the stained-glass windows. Guy recognised the faces all around him, people he'd known since childhood: Father Gaufre's massive red face, Billault the bell ringer's black moustache. In the congregation he saw his aunts, his cousins, every remaining Hardelot from the region that ran from the English Channel to Arras on one side and the Belgian border to Paris on the other. And here, too, were the younger generation, who lived in Lille or Calais: the women wore make-up, elegant suits, beautiful fur coats over their Flemish bodies, heavy breasts and wide hips. The older men were also present, with their beards, pince-nez, black frock coats and a slight family resemblance in their features; they were rivals in business, brought long, drawn-out court cases against each other, argued over legacies eaten up by the taxman; they were malicious, suspicious of each other, but in spite of everything they were united in circumstances such as these, even when the departed had nothing much to leave.

Colette had gone with her brother to pay her respects to the dead woman; she was to stay for two days. 'She's the spitting image of Marthe Hardelot,' everyone said. She looked sweet and young, not very clever, with pink cheeks, brown eyes and a warm, shy expression.

Both Guy and Colette felt nervous at being back in Saint-Elme.

'This hideous hole,' thought Guy. 'I hope I never see the place again.'

Opposite him he could see Simone Burgères and Rose; the young woman was tall and beautiful, he thought vaguely. There was seven years' difference in age between him and Rose; it was the first time he had actually seen her. But he looked at her with hostility: she was part of a different clan, the enemy, the daughter of Simone, who had ruined him, and of ... Ah, he didn't like recalling that time, that man. He had never seen his mistress again. He wasn't in love with her any more; he had forgotten her. But that man, no, he still hadn't forgiven him. The memory of the first betrayal wounds the pride more than the heart and fades more slowly.

Once the ceremony was over, everyone went back home, back to the warm fire and set table with that feeling of comfort and joy you have after a long walk in the rain, or when you've buried someone whose life and death are equally meaningless to you. Everyone in Saint-Elme was talking about Colette and Guy Hardelot. They had waited with great curiosity for the moment when the Burgères and the Hardelots would come face to face as they all filed by to offer their condolences. And, at the Hardelot-Demestres' house, it was announced that the next day Guy would be invited to visit the Burgères.

'How do you know that, Grandfather?'

Hardelot-Demestre always knew everything. He was an old man with slim shoulders and a white beard. He walked slowly through the dining room, round the cleared table, rubbing his dry hands together and smiling, with a gleam in his eye, making everyone beg him to tell them what he knew. He had seen Madame Burgères's maid hand a note to Madame Florent's maid and, also, the Burgères's car had been seen going to the next town to buy food, which was only ever done the day before they were having dinner guests. 'Ah, the Burgères don't throw their money out of the window,' people said with respect. In these old families of Saint-Elme, people admired thriftiness as much as they did wealth: both were prime virtues, the cornerstones on which a family's prosperity was built. While they were talking, the radio was broadcasting the world news. Everything was unstable, falling apart; it seemed as if the clatter of swords, the tramping of boots, the distant rumble of marching armies could be heard even in this peaceful Saint-Elme sitting room. At the home of the Hardelot-Demestres they discussed the dowry of Rose Burgères. The young woman would be twenty-one in 1941.

'Her mother will marry her off while she's young; they don't get along,' people said.

The next day Guy and Colette were indeed invited to the Burgères house. It was a small dinner party, because of the mourning period, but Saint-Elme was meant to know that the former and new proprietors of the factory were on good terms. All the bad feeling between them was masked by these subtle details of behaviour: just as the sludge at the bottom of a lake is hidden by clear, sparkling water.

Colette was very happy to be invited to dinner; she put on lipstick, though the girls in Saint-Elme never wore make-up. Two of Rose's female cousins were also invited; they wore dark-brown taffeta dresses with high collars; their necks and cheeks were shiny, and they looked at Colette with envy, consoling themselves with the thought of their dowries, for they all knew that this little Hardelot girl . . . After dinner Madame Burgères sat down in an armchair, her knitting on her lap and some official papers on a table in front of her. She looked them over and knitted at the same time; she was using thin, rough wool to make clothes for the workers' children. Sometimes she would stop, put down her knitting needles and pick up a red pencil to make notes in the margins of the letters.

The young people sat on stiff chairs, talking quietly. Rose was saying she'd be coming to Paris in the spring.

'You must come and see us,' said Guy, sounding so eager that his sister was surprised. 'Will you be staying long?'

'Oh, as long as possible,' she replied.

'Poor girl,' thought Guy. 'Her life can't be much fun.'

She was dressed rather badly, in a fabric that was too sumptuous and too dark, and made her look old; her full mouth and thick eyebrows gave her an almost harsh look, but there was something about her that Guy liked. He couldn't say exactly what . . . the way she moved her lips when she spoke or laughed, a glimmer of intelligence and daring in her eyes. He looked over at the young Renaudin girls, who secretly glanced at him tenderly, languorously. Their voices had risen slightly: when a young man is with an innocent young girl, she shows her emotions this way, in spite of herself, just as a pussycat miaows more shrilly than usual when she spots a tomcat. Rose didn't say very much; she lowered her eyes but Guy could sense that she was watching him and it pleased him.

The clock struck eleven. Madame Burgères folded away her knitting. Colette and Guy said goodbye. Madame Burgères offered to drive them home, but no, they wanted to walk. They knew very well that people from good families never set foot outside after dark in Saint-Elme and they got illicit pleasure from breaking these sacrosanct rules.

Guy shook Rose's hand.

She looked up at him. 'Will I see you again?' she asked.

She had spoken quickly and quietly. Nothing was more attractive to Guy than a courageous young woman, and he understood how brave she must be to ask him that with her mother listening. 'They must keep a close eye on her,' he thought to himself, 'she's the heiress.'

He liked her more and more. He smiled. 'Come and see Colette tomorrow,' he said. 'We can talk about it some more then. Will you come?'

'Yes.'

'You have to go to Saint-Omer with me tomorrow, Rose,' Madame Burgères said suddenly from her chair.

'Tomorrow? But you said Saturday.'

'It's tomorrow.'

'Come in the morning,' Colette whispered in her friend's ear.

The young people left. Soft, light snow was falling from the dark skies. Saint-Elme was asleep. All the shutters were closed, the doors locked. In Jault's Inn, the workers drank beer, and music rose from a player piano. Colette and Guy walked past their old house; it still had a 'For Sale' sign on the balcony.

'Nothing in the world would make me come back here,' said Colette. 'What about you?'

Guy didn't reply.

# 22

Everyone waited for the war to start the way people wait for death: knowing it is inevitable, asking only for a little more time. 'I'm aware you can't be avoided, Death, but wait a bit, wait until I've finished building my house, planting this tree, seen my son married, wait until I no longer want to live.' It was the same with the war: they asked for no more than time. A few more months of peace, another year, one more sweet, carefree summer ... Nothing more. They wanted tomorrow to be just like today, with soup on the table, the family all together, amusements, work, love, just a bit more time, just a few more moments. Then ... It was like in old paintings where Death walks beside a labourer pushing his plough, Death drinks from a rich man's cup, sleeps on a poor man's thin mattress, sings with musicians at feasts, holds court at church, in humble cottages, in palaces: so, in 1938, people sensed the constant presence of war, invisible yet all around them. Death took them by the hand and led them where it pleased; it made their food horribly bitter, poisoned their pleasures; Death stood at their side as they leaned over the cradles of newborn children.

And still people carried on living as they always had. They hosted grand dinners where black-suited Jeremiahs carved the pheasant, sliced the truffled foie gras and imagined future wars as if they were right in the middle of them. 'A sudden invasion, one day, at dawn, the airfields bombed . . . civilians machine-gunned down along the roads . . .' The women shook their heads and murmured, 'Awful, just awful . . .' while thinking, 'I should have worn my pink dress. How annoying . . . I'm underdressed.' They were predicting the Cabinet would collapse on Monday. The maids served the ice cream on crystal dishes with little gold-plated spoons. Someone announced that a trustworthy source had told him that Hitler would be sending his troops to the Ukraine in the spring. There was fighting in Spain. People got married, died, brought children into the world. In the Hardelot and Burgères households great confusion reigned, for Guy wanted to marry Rose.

The Hardelots thought it was a godsend, yet, in spite of that, they were not happy about it; they didn't like the idea that their son might want Rose's dowry. Madame Burgères declared she would never consent to the marriage. Rose had spent nearly three months in Paris and had seen Guy every day. She had returned to Saint-Elme and announced she was engaged. It was a harsh blow to Simone. Those Hardelots again! Now Agnès's son would one day be the owner of the factory. Rose was only eighteen, fortunately. Her mother still controlled her. But it was no longer a time when a girl was locked up, forced to get married. Yes, Simone controlled the fortune, of course, but she also feared a scandal more than almost anything else. Her good reputation in Saint-Elme meant a lot to her. She did not wish to be accused of depriving her daughter of her money, or of being a bad mother. And all the old gossip she thought had been forgotten resurfaced. People were talking about her broken engagement, so long ago. They said she had never forgiven Pierre and Agnès their happi-ness, their love, that she had got her revenge by ruining them, that she hated Rose. There were even whispers that she had encouraged Burgères to seduce Guy's mistress, to make the young man desperate. So it was that Saint-Elme invented the darkest of plots, its inhabitants trying to guess what was going on in the Burgères household. Its comings and goings were even discussed in the workers' cottages, having first been recounted to the female cousins of the Renaudins, who then passed the information on to old Monsieur Hardelot-Demestre. The elderly Madame Florent felt young again, going from one house to another with her black umbrella (it was the rainy season) and her large bulging handbag containing two pairs of glasses, her keys and a handkerchief with a black border (she wore mourning for all those who had died in the Hardelot family, just as in England the shopkeepers dress in black whenever a member of the royal family dies). She insinuated that Simone Burgères was keeping her daughter shut away. She spread the rumour, vague and imprecise, that there would be a scandal, and whenever she came across Rose on the streets of Saint-Elme she would go up to her, look at her, tears in her eyes and whisper, 'You poor thing, you poor girl ...' Then she would kiss her on both cheeks and walk away, pretending to wipe her tears. Despite Simone expressly forbidding it, Rose often went to see the elderly Madame Florent, who told her (in her own way) about Pierre's and Agnès's marriage.

'In those days,' she said, 'young women weren't free, the way they are now. Marriages were arranged by the parents in good families (and the Florents are an excellent family) and the young people simply had to accept it. Agnès was engaged to a very rich, handsome and distinguished gentleman. But she was in love with Pierre Hardelot. Fortunately, she adored me, so she hid nothing from me. "Darling Mama," she said to me one day, "you are so intelligent, you understand everything ... You are my very best friend. Give me your advice. What should I do? Should I ignore my heart and marry the man you have chosen for me?" – "No," I told her, "no, my darling child, I have lived for you

alone and I want you to be happy. A marriage where the heart
is silenced is a caricature of conjugal love. Money, the frivolous
things in life are meaningless without deep, reciprocal love. If
you love Pierre Hardelot, you must marry him." And so she
asked to meet him in the Coudre Woods. "Listen," she told him,
"I have both my mother and my conscience on my side. I have
broken my engagement. I will follow you to the ends of the
earth." The young couple were determined to run away together,
just like in *The Beautiful Love Affair*, a charming play, my dear
Rose; haven't you heard of it? When I learned what they intended
to do, my heart missed a beat. I wasted not a moment. I went
to see Pierre Hardelot's parents (his mother was an excellent
creature, not terribly intelligent, but a homemaker, with a good
heart). "So, we're going to sort this out, aren't we?" I said. "Let
his grandfather scream and shout; he'll come round to it once
their first child is born! Let us make these children happy." I
spoke with great authority, which won these good people over
and, upon my word, Pierre and Agnès were married two months
later. But it takes a strong will, determination, you can't let yourself be led along like a child, damn it. Sometimes you must risk
everything in life. You have to fight for your happiness,' she said
and pushed her tapestry needle into her embroidery with a look
of triumph.

It was the beginning of August. Anxious people everywhere
turned their attention towards Spain, or China, or Czechoslovakia.
But Czechoslovakia seemed the least threatening. Lord Runciman
was in Prague where everything had been arranged for him to
work, to enjoy himself and to act as mediator in the conflict over
the Sudetenland. 'That will buy time until the autumn,' people
said, 'so we can get the harvest in; wars never start in autumn;
everybody knows that.' 'Indeed,' said the elderly Hardelot-
Demestre, 'in '14 it started a month too late.' It was unanimous;
spring was the dangerous time. Come now, they thought, 1938

would carry on and finish its course without terror becoming a reality.

A month and a half later, when everyone was waiting with bated breath for the results of Chamberlain's talks with Hitler, Madame Florent was leaning out of her window, trying to catch a glimpse of the gate into the Burgères's grounds. She had sent a little note to Rose. 'I must speak to you, my darling. Be brave and trust me.' The whiff of danger excites the elderly, imbues them with strength; except when it doesn't have the opposite effect of killing them with anxiety. Perhaps this is because they do not feel that they alone are threatened by death: a sense of equality is re-established between them and the rest of the world. Madame Florent, hearing the distant rumble of the cannons heading towards the border, quivered with warrior-like passion. The current situation brought undreamed-of opportunities to arrange a marriage between Guy and Rose. Rose was a determined girl, with a lively, fighting spirit, but she was still so young . . . Would she dare stand up to her mother, to society? And yet, so much was at stake. 'The happiness of a lifetime,' thought the elderly woman: the factory won back and she herself, Madame Florent, in her twilight years, recovering the respect, the envy and the admiration of Saint-Elme. Nostalgically she recalled the happy days gone by (the ones after the reconciliation of grandfather Hardelot and his grandson). There wasn't a wedding between Calais and Arras that Madame Florent hadn't been invited to after that. And so many visits at New Year, from really the most respected people in the area. She sighed. Finally, she saw Rose walking towards her along the road. She waved to her from the window and let her in, welcoming her with open arms.

'Well, my dear girl, is there to be a war?' she asked as they went into the sitting room.

Rose stood next to her, tight lipped, eyes sparkling. 'I received a letter from . . .' she whispered finally. She couldn't bring herself to say Guy's name. She burst into tears, fell sobbing on to a chair, biting its grey slipcover to muffle the sound of her crying.

The elderly Madame Florent raised her eyes towards heaven; she had a way of rolling them upwards beneath her heavy, ageing eyelids that gave her a fleeting resemblance to a bulldog.

'My poor darling . . .' she said. 'There's nothing to be done. But it's awful. To be separated like this, in the prime of youth, and for how long? Alas, the war will be long, the war will be harsh. But in one way it's perhaps better that this is happening now, while you're still only engaged. For just imagine how painful it would be for a young wife . . .'

Rose broke in. 'Oh, don't say that, Madame. If we could live together just for one day, for one hour! And then . . . there would be memories, just think of it, memories that would last a lifetime. But this way, to lose him before I've had the joy of being his wife. I love him so much, Madame, I do love him. He told me he'll be among the first to go, he's said goodbye to me. Oh, I want to see him again, I'm begging you, what should I do? If he comes to Saint-Elme, Mama would keep me locked away. Listen, Madame . . .'

She dried her eyes.

'I want to leave. I want to get away from here,' she said, her voice trembling and breaking with emotion. 'Yes, I'll go to Paris. After that my mother will be forced to give her consent. That's what you would tell me to do, isn't it, Madame? Listen, there's a train leaving at three fifty-five. I'll go straight from here to the station. Only, the thing is, I have no money. My mother has refused to give me my allowance this month, so I can't even buy a stamp without her knowing. But you'll lend me enough money for a ticket to Paris, won't you? Oh, Madame, I'm coming to you as your daughter Agnès did before, begging . . . begging you, "You are so intelligent; you understand everything!"'

Madame Florent hesitated only a second. 'I was born to be a great leader,' she thought with pride.

'You have to risk your all,' she said, 'that's my advice. You should go.'

She gave her the money she needed, walked her to the garden gate, watched her run towards the station. Then she put on her hat and went to tell all of Saint-Elme what had just happened.

# 23

As soon as morning came that day, all the sensible people began leaving Paris. The rain continued to fall. Everywhere, women came out of their houses, arms full of packages and children. They looked up at the sky with questioning eyes, either trying to find a glimmer of hope from above, or spot the first enemy plane, it was difficult to say which. Those who couldn't make up their minds telephoned each other: 'What are you going to do? Are you leaving?' and faltering voices replied with feigned indifference: 'Oh, if it were up to me, you know . . . if I were the only one to consider . . . the idea wouldn't even cross my mind, my dear friend. But there are the children (or my sick mother, my father, my younger sister . . .).' On all the roads leading away from Paris, cars headed for the peaceful regions of central France. They didn't drive overly fast: panic had not yet set in; they weren't actually very afraid. It was caution that led them far from the threatened capital. The roofs of powerful luxury automobiles were piled high with luggage; old family cars had birdcages hanging from the window and two or three babies asleep in the back. The men who had been called up to fight carried small suitcases and made their way to the train stations. On the Boulevard de Courcelles, where the Hardelots lived, the shops were locking up;

women, eyes red from crying, hung notices on the metal shutters:
'Closed due to mobilisation'. Agnès was packing for Pierre and
Guy; Guy was joining his regiment; Pierre had decided to go to
Saint-Elme, to try to talk things through with Simone and convince
her to agree to an official engagement between Guy and her
daughter.

Rose had arrived at the Hardelots' house the night before, trembling with fear, pride and love. 'Don't send me back,' she had
said. 'I've run away. I wanted to see Guy before he leaves.'

'My poor child,' cried Agnès, 'what have you done?'

'What *you* did when you were young, Madame. *You* married
the man you loved. *You* weren't afraid of upsetting your family:
you can't send me away, you just can't.'

They were moved by her words and especially by seeing Guy
so happy. Knowing that Guy would be leaving the next day, they
were prepared to give their lives for him and even more prepared
to take responsibility for any foolish acts their son might commit.
They went into the next room, leaving the young couple alone.

'This is so awful,' Pierre said over and over again, 'so awful . . .
Good Lord . . . There are going to be hideous complications to
face.'

'But he'll go away happy,' said Agnès. 'Pierre, my darling love,
I would have done exactly the same for you, thirty years ago.'

'But Simone will never agree to this marriage.'

'She'll have to now, or there'll be such a scandal . . .'

'Yes, but Rose has very little money of her own. If her mother
doesn't give in . . .'

'What can we do?' said Agnès. 'They can come and live here.'

Her husband looked at her. 'You've never been jealous where
Guy is concerned. It's odd.'

She shook her head. 'I have loved you too much to be jealous
of my children, my old darling. We've had a good life; we've
been happy. Now it's their turn.'

'Happy,' he murmured bitterly, pointing at Guy's suitcase, at the sweater and socks, the chocolate and sugar, and the bottle of medicinal alcohol Agnès had laid out on the bed before packing them for his departure, 'happy, when for the second time . . .'

Agnès's hands were shaking, but she said nothing. He turned away, muttered, 'I'll go and find out what's happening.'

In the sitting room Guy and Rose were on the settee, talking quietly, their faces anguished but radiant with love. Pierre remembered how his son had lain dying on a hospital bed, over a woman he had now forgotten; he shrugged his shoulders, switched on the radio, buried his head in his hands and listened to the news of the negotiations between various governments. It wasn't good. Another night of torture. And Guy would leave tomorrow.

He refused to allow Agnès to go to the station with their son. 'You can remember what it was like, can't you? It's no place for a woman. It will be him and me, just the two of us.'

But when they came out of the Métro station he couldn't bring himself to go any further. Suddenly, he was overwhelmed by a moment of weakness. He recovered his composure with difficulty, patted his son on the back and leaned against his shoulder. Guy was a head taller than him. 'Don't worry, my boy.'

'I'm not, Papa. Everything will die down, you'll see. But there's Rose . . .'

'Yes. Don't worry. I'll go and see Simone tonight.'

'Make sure she understands that we won't change our minds. We'll just wait until Rose is twenty-one, that's all.'

'Yes. I know.'

They hugged each other. He watched his son walk away and disappear into the crowd. Then head down, dragging one leg along behind him, he stepped into the street. People were waiting for newspapers to be delivered to the empty stands and, even though they didn't know each other, they started conversations.

'That's a bad sign,' thought Pierre, 'a bad sign.'

He didn't want to wait for the newspapers. He had no hope left. He climbed on to a bus. A large gentleman was talking loudly, saying he had it on good authority 'that the King of Italy would abdicate if his country declared war'. People shook their heads.

'It's no surprise, coming from Victor Emmanuel,' the large gentleman said proudly. 'I've always held him in the utmost esteem.'

The rain kept falling.

After having lunch, Pierre said goodbye to his family and left for Saint-Elme. It was nine o'clock when he arrived at Simone's house. He waited for a long time in the dimly lit room, next to the yellow lamp with a bronze stand that he knew so well. It had been handed down from one of the Renaudin grandmothers and whenever he had been to see Simone on those formal visits during their engagement they had sat next to each other, beside this lamp, in silence, while the chaperones (poor Marthe and an elderly female cousin of Simone's) had sat in armchairs, watching them with an expression that was both affectionate and mistrustful at the same time. The memory of those times had been so odious for so long; yet now, it seemed almost sweet and comical. Pierre pushed his fingers through his hair several times; he was going grey. My God, how quickly time passed. How terrifying and strange it was . . .

He was so immersed in thoughts of the past that he jumped when he saw Simone. He had hardly recognised the heavy woman in her black dress. He walked over to her and took her hand. 'Simone, I understand how angry you are, but . . .'

She cut in. 'More suffering because of you and your family,' she said. She was utterly furious. 'You bring me nothing but bad luck. Wasn't it enough that everything was your fault, everything that's happened to me all my life?'

She was choking; she covered her mouth with her handkerchief. 'Tell Rose to stay where she is. I never want to see her again. Let her marry your son. She's never to set foot here again. I will not congratulate you; you won't have an easy daughter-in-law. A young woman capable of defying her mother will not make a good wife. But she'll get along with your wife, no doubt. You . . .'

He tried to calm her down. 'There is nothing to reproach her about. She disobeyed you, it's true, but her reputation has not been ruined. As soon as she arrived at the station she came straight to our house. And ever since then she has been looked after by my wife.'

'Your wife! Don't talk to me about your wife. I . . .'

She stopped herself, then continued. 'I hate her,' she said more quietly, her voice icy with rage, 'and everything to do with her. Her son, even you, who belong to her and her alone. I . . .'

'But you loved me once,' he said, looking with pity at her enormous, pale, tear-stained face. 'We're old, Simone, all that is in the past. How can you still be so resentful over something that happened so long ago?'

'It feels like yesterday,' she whispered.

'You got married. You didn't mourn for long. You were happy.'

'Married for my money,' she said bitterly. 'Cheated on, abandoned, and him, dying with your son's mistress. I'm telling you, you bring me nothing but suffering. Rose can do what she likes. I know her; she won't give in. Keep her. Let them get married. But she'd better not expect anything from me. You know she has no money. She can wait until I die, if she likes. But as long as I live . . .'

'It's nothing to do with money,' he said coldly.

They had moved apart. They looked at each other with hatred. A beam of light scanned the dark sky, looking for enemy planes. Pierre's heart was pierced by the thought of how, perhaps at that very moment, war had been declared and his son would be leaving. If Rose could bring Guy some happiness, even if only when he was home on leave, even for forty-eight hours or one night, nothing else mattered.

'Guy has been called up,' he said. 'He left this morning. You don't have a son. You can't understand. We ask nothing of you except your consent. Rose can live with us. Will you oppose their marriage?'

'No,' she replied.

'All right, then . . .'

He bowed and started to leave the sitting room. In silence, she walked him to the door and switched on the large white lamp that lit up the street. He found himself once more in Saint-Elme; the town was darker and more silent than ever, asleep beneath the rain.

# 24

'I'm not jealous of *her*,' Agnès said to her husband, once they were in their room and could talk, while 'the children' sat together in the sitting room and made them, the parents, feel like intruders. 'I'm not jealous of *her*, *she's* jealous of me.'

'*She*' was Rose, Guy Hardelot's wife of just a few weeks.

'If they could have their own apartment, things would be easier,' replied Pierre as he slowly undressed next to the large bed where Agnès was lying, 'but everything is so expensive.'

Guy was earning two thousand eight hundred francs a month. Simone Burgères had kept her word: Rose had no dowry. Pierre Hardelot was financially responsible for the young couple. After a brief honeymoon in the Midi, they had to make do with one room in the apartment on the Boulevard de Courcelles. Rose immediately began to feel she had lost what was rightfully hers and, far from lessening as the days went by, this feeling grew more painful and bitter. Being controlled by her mother had seemed hideous to her; she'd felt that nothing could be more lovely or pleasant than living with the Hardelots. But this was not the case. Even though Pierre and Agnès did their very best to remain in the background, everything reminded Rose that they were in charge: where they sat at the dining table, the menus Agnès chose, the grudging way the maid reacted if Rose asked her to stop doing the housework in the morning and iron one of her nightdresses; most especially, the tender deference Guy displayed towards his family. All these things were constant reminders to Rose of the situation she had been forced into. She did not regret her marriage; she loved Guy with a passion that was exclusive and jealous. But it was exactly because of her ardour and jealousy that she wanted her husband to herself, and to herself alone.

'I can't show my love for you freely here,' she would say when they were in bed, their warm, trembling young bodies holding each other tightly in the darkness. 'I feel embarrassed. I feel as if Colette and your mother are listening through the wall.'

'Don't be silly; that's madness,' he'd reply.

Yet he too was trying to find a way to change their lives. But how could they live even reasonably well on two thousand eight hundred francs a month?

'Your father could give us an allowance,' whispered Rose.

Guy knew that his father didn't have enough money to support two households. There was nothing to be done, they simply had to wait.

'Look, my parents are wonderful, they are so fond of you,' he would say as he stroked his wife's strong white neck.

Then she would start to cry. Her tears dripped on to Guy's bare chest. In the next room Agnès could hear them whispering; she could make out the odd word, an annoyed cry from Rose, stifled by kisses. Her daughter-in-law's animosity aroused the same feeling in Agnès. One look, a single awkward word, caused icy tension between them. If Rose said something rude, Agnès would snap back at her. Even her voice changed when she was speaking to Rose; her normally measured, sweet tone became shriller, more nervous and clipped. She realised that she was beginning to hate Rose, just as in the past her mother-in-law, deep down, had undoubtedly secretly hated her.

'How can you say that? Mama was always so nice to you,' Pierre said reproachfully.

'Oh, *you* thought everything your parents did was perfect,' she replied.

Then, because she realised when something was ridiculous, she thought about how she was parroting the discussions between her son and her daughter-in-law and she laughed at herself, but with a hint of bitterness.

So they staggered forward towards summer one day at a time. Beneath the rain and cold wind, the famous Longchamps Races closed the season in Paris. The Hardelots left for Wimereux. Guy's holidays began in August, and he and his wife had been invited to stay with friends at Ciboure. But within a few days he received a call to return to the factory in Paris. The colleague who was standing in for him needed an emergency operation. The setback would be temporary and Guy hoped to be back in Ciboure by 25 August.

With their espadrilles drying on the terrace, Guy and Rose lay naked in the sun, their bodies dusted with sand. Guy grabbed a handful of sweet, moist tamarisk flowers, pressed them to his cheek and smiled. He explained to Rose why she shouldn't be so foolish as to go back to Paris with him.

'We'll be apart ten days, two weeks at the most. Firmin,' (that was the name of the other engineer at the factory) 'Firmin gets back from his holiday on the 23rd and will take over from me. Think of the cost of two journeys.'

She found him annoyingly logical. Nevertheless, she felt it was a point of honour not to let him see how disappointed she was. Reluctantly, she let him leave.

Right up until the last moment, neither Guy nor Rose believed there would be a war. The year before, war had seemed possible. They had been separated; they had been miserable; the world could be coming to an end. But now that everything was going well, that they were living together, they were husband and wife, they expected everything around them to be as peaceful and loving as it was within them. The news that Guy was being called up again was the worst thing they could imagine.

'Once more, because of *their* dirty war, you're going to miss out on your holiday, my beloved . . .' wrote Rose.

In Wimereux the Hardelots invited the Hardelot-Demestres from Saint-Elme to come to dinner. Over dessert, they all agreed: it was impossible that there would be a war this year – the Germans had no train carriages left. Everything would calm down again but mobilisation was unavoidable. There had already been two rounds of conscription. Once again the shops in Paris were closing; they lowered the iron shutters, tearing down notices that said 'Closed due to holidays' and replacing them with new ones that read 'Closed due to mobilisation'. One sceptic had even written 'annual mobilisation'.

At the seaside the weather had been overcast and unsettled, but now it was beautiful. The sun glistened on the little white notices (every day new ones appeared on the gilded walls of the town hall); the conscripts were being called up one after another. The tanned faces of the women grew furrowed with anguish beneath their creams and make-up. Villas were closed up. Spanish children with large dark eyes ruled alone on the burning beach and streets. All the French were leaving. They hastily packed their damp swimming costumes and sandy sandals into their suitcases, and the women shed tears into the folds of organdie dresses they had carefully set aside to wear on September evenings.

During the long, calm, beautiful evenings, as crickets chirped in the gardens and the moon shone brightly on the old sea wall, Rose and her friends (whose husbands were also young and had been called up) sat in the living room of the villa, waiting to hear the latest news on the radio. The atmosphere of anxiety and apprehension was becoming more and more stifling. The nervous women pretended to be sewing or knitting, but their trembling fingers tore the wool, dropped the needles. Nevertheless, each of them found causes for hope in something they'd read in the newspaper, in the radio presenter's voice, in the letter they'd received the day before. All their absent husbands seemed to have passed the word on; they wrote the same thing. 'Things will die down again. Nothing will happen here. Just stay calm, my darling.'

The women dared not disobey, even though they knew they were being lied to, that the men wanted them to stay far away from the danger in Paris. Life was no longer normal; it was nightmarish, a series of grotesque, deformed images. The Spanish cook brought a salad of mixed peppers to the table and burst into tears. She was married to a Frenchman; it was war, he was leaving. Eagerly, they turned the dial on the radio and heard gypsy love songs from Budapest. Beneath the moonlight, cats miaowed, ran across the rooftops, played on the shiny white gravel. The sweet scent of flowers wafted in through the open windows. The sea was cool, soothing, innocent. The women looked over at the empty wicker chairs on the terrace, where, a week before, the men they loved had been smoking, laughing, reading the paper. They thought of the large bed beneath the mosquito net. Under the cushions on the settee, they found a lost cigarette, a bit of warm sand, and felt they were already widows.

At the beginning of a catastrophe one thinks of others. No one wanted to worry or upset anyone else. They lowered their voices, tried to sound calm. They talked about meaningless things: the weather, their morning swim, their clothes. Then, after a moment's silence, one of them would feign indifference and ask, 'By the way, what did Guy tell you this morning?'

And Rose, eyes lowered, her voice choking with despair, read out the letter that she knew by heart.

'I am convinced that everything will be all right again. Every day I meet people who have the most up-to-date information; they all agree with me. It will end as it did last September, because, basically, no one wants war. In any case, don't come back here; that would be silly.'

The women clung on to his words: 'Every day I meet people who have the most up-to-date information . . .' They imagined what they looked like, these serious, solemn men who knew everything, who could predict everything, even the most secret thoughts of their leaders, who had looked deep into their hearts and dreams, and were confident there would be no war. They had to believe them. Yet the news grew worse from hour to hour. It seemed as if the very air they breathed was gradually becoming thinner and thinner. They were suffocating from a feeling of anxiety that was both deadly and cruel.

In the small sitting room the women didn't speak; the clock slowly ticked. On the radio, a waltz was cut short, as if it had suddenly dropped down into an abyss. A moment of silence . . . their hearts seemed to stop beating. Rose was playing with her brand-new wedding ring, holding it in her hands, stroking it, studying it; then came the presenter's voice: 'Here is a broadcast from French radio . . .' The programme ended. 'Well, nothing new,' murmured a voice. Someone else said, 'No . . . still nothing.' Rose suddenly stood up, threw a coat over her light dress and went down to the beach. Through the damp night, a semicircle of lights shimmered around the bay. In front of the terrace of a café a group of people stood motionless in the darkness, waiting for the next radio broadcast.

It was the same every day until the order came for general mobilisation. A little girl shouted out from her garden, 'Mama, can you hear the bells? Is it a holiday?' Women wept openly on the streets.

The men were calm, some of them laughed. 'So! It was inevitable. Here we go again,' they said, shrugging their shoulders.

Rose, who had tried in vain to telephone Paris, came back from the post office dry-eyed, pale, trembling, and looking ten years older. 'I'm leaving tonight,' she said. 'I should get there just in time. He's not going until the day after tomorrow.'

Already everything had changed so dramatically that this twenty-four-hour delay felt like a blessing. Twenty-four hours . . . So much could happen in twenty-four hours, so many kisses, so many tears, such bitter, intense pleasures.

Rose was on the last 'civilian' train. There weren't many women. The mobilised soldiers were heading for their units. Men slept in the corridors, sat perched on packing cases; farmers drank wine in silence, wiped clean the windows with their sleeves and looked out at the farms and little railway stations. Bourgeois and worker spoke to each other, gesticulating energetically. You could catch certain words: 'Hitler . . . Italy . . . England . . . Munich . . .' The farmers either said nothing or spoke quietly among themselves about everyday life, the life they still clung to, the life they would keep with them, hold on to throughout war, or captivity, until the day they died, as if it were the very flesh that covered their bones. '. . . The cow . . . the potatoes . . . the fruit . . . we got a lot this year, a lot . . .' They passed trees laden with peaches. 'Ain't it awful to see 'em all go to waste,' they said, 'but the women will see to them . . .'

A frail man with worried eyes kept saying over and over again, 'They called me up. I'm going, but I'm too old to be a soldier. I was in the other one, from 1914 to 1919, in the Dardanelles . . .' The other one . . . the other war . . . People said these words in a stunned tone of voice: it was a new phrase. Another war . . . Twice in one lifetime, it was too much. But everyone was bowed beneath the same destiny, and courage was born out of their communal ordeal.

'Are you going to Paris?' an old woman asked Rose. 'Is it true we're going to be bombed? Aren't you afraid?'

She shook her head, 'no'. The past and the present were strangely and sadly confused in her mind. There was no distinct break: the hopes, habits, feelings, desires of the past clung to her like a bleeding limb that is being amputated, but whose nerves, flesh, muscles remain painfully attached to the body. She looked up at the clear, beautiful sky. 'When he gets his holiday it will be hot,' she thought, then, 'But no . . . he's going away . . . We're at war.' When she opened her handbag and took out a bit of bread and some fruit she'd brought, for she hadn't had lunch and was starving, she found a sample of printed silk. She had ordered a dress to be sent to her, but now she might never wear it, he might never see it.

'Why are you going to Paris?' the old woman asked with curiosity.

'I want to see my husband,' she replied.

'Well, *I'm* going to get my sheets,' said the old woman. 'What if the house is bombed, just think of it. Sheets that belonged to my mother.'

Everyone who could remember the other war was talking about it. 'It won't be the same, this time. We're strong now . . . we have cannons and planes.'

When the train stopped at the stations, people leaned out of the windows; they looked at the soldiers guarding the tracks with curiosity; the moonlight lit up their helmets and belts, making them shine, and the barrels of their rifles gleamed with a bluish light. Convoys of women and children fleeing Paris headed for the centre of France. The train started off again. In the starlit skies, people looked for the first planes.

Rose slept for a few hours. When she woke up it was daybreak. Some horses were walking through a village.

'They're requisitioning them,' someone said.

Like a millstone constantly in motion, the idea of war crushed their hearts. At every moment you could see it, you could breathe it; war was present in every action, every word, every thought.

At the station in Paris the trains were besieged by mobs of people, children were passed through the windows of the packed compartments. By contrast, the streets were calm. But nowhere could the soul find a moment's respite; everything evoked the same thought: 'We're at war . . . war . . . war . . .'

Passers-by held gas masks in their hands, but apart from that, nothing had changed. Flowers were sold on the street corners. Housewives bought cherries. Children ran about. At the door of her house Rose stopped, her heart pounding; she looked up for a moment at the window of her bedroom on the third floor. She was suddenly worried that Guy might scold her for coming back. Slowly she climbed the stairs; the lift wasn't working. She rang the bell. She could hear Guy's footsteps on the bare floor. She closed her eyes so she could hear him more clearly, so the sound was engraved in her mind, never to be forgotten. She imagined that she would throw herself into his arms, hold him close and cry out, 'Don't go! I don't want you to go. I want to keep you with me.' But war was already hardening everyone's soul. So when the door opened she smiled at him and said softly, 'It's me. Don't be angry.'

Then she took off her hat and asked, 'Is it really war this time?'

He looked at her in silence.

It really was war.

# 25

The men had gone. There had been no shouting, no singing, no flowers. Their children had gone. All alone, the women did their women's chores. They organised the house; they put the summer clothes in trunks up in the attic. Rose, Agnès and Colette were working together. Agnès and Colette had come back from Wimereux a few hours before Guy left. They didn't cry. The war was already trying to create its own legend. It was understood that the women had to prove themselves worthy of the soldiers through their calmness, their courage, their blind confidence that fate would smile on them. For Agnès it was easier; she had played this role before. For four years she had lowered her head, waited, fought back her tears in silence, smiled at young and old; she had hoped. But for the younger women it was all much harder. Stubborn, anxious, passionate, they had believed until now that it was easy to control their destiny. Rose had felt proud of her strength and youth: running away from home, refusing to obey her mother, marrying the man she chose. And here she was, defeated, having lost everything. She felt hopeless rage, a blinding bitterness that encompassed the entire universe. Alone in her room, she shook her fist at the blue sky. How high and luminous it was, this summer sky. Pigeons cooed on the balcony. Evening came slowly, so slowly. Like blind fish drifting through transparent water, the silver barrage balloons floated up into the green-gold air. Agnès was taping on to the windows the strips of paper that people hoped would provide some protection from the falling bombs. Rose was lying on her unmade metal bed, biting into the pillow to muffle her sobs.

Colette went into her sister-in-law's room. 'Come on, my dear Rose, don't stay in here. Come on . . .'

Rose looked at her and shook her head. 'How I envy you. How lucky you are. *You* don't have anyone out there!'

'But there's Guy . . .'

'Oh, a brother, what's a brother? It's sad, of course, and I know you love him. But Colette, if you only knew how I . . .'

In a sudden movement that made Colette blush and seemed almost improper, Rose struck her bare breasts with her fists. 'I feel as if my heart is being torn out,' she said more quietly.

Colette threw herself down on to her knees beside the bed. 'There isn't only Guy,' she said, holding Rose's hand and pressing it to her cheek, 'there's someone else . . .'

Rose wasn't listening. Only one love counted for her: her own. Gradually, she calmed down. She didn't want to hurt Colette's feelings. 'Someone else?' she asked apathetically.

Colette whispered a name. 'You don't know him,' she added. 'I met him last winter. We met at Wimereux. In that godforsaken place, it was inevitable, you can see that; we were always to-gether . . . But it would have remained just a friendship, a deep friendship, if it hadn't been for those last few days . . . those last few hours . . . And so, he said . . . he said . . .' She lowered her eyes, toyed nervously with a little gold bracelet she was wearing. 'He said . . . "I can't live without you . . ." and we got engaged,' she concluded, her voice trembling.

She waited for Rose to reply.

'Congratulations, darling,' said Rose automatically, all the while thinking, 'Why is she talking about engagement and love? How can she possibly understand? Only Guy and I know, only we really know.'

But she gave Colette a light kiss on the cheek. 'I'm very happy for you,' she said.

'But he's gone,' said Colette softly. 'He'll come back, I'm sure of that, he'll come back. Intuition, you know . . . it's usually right, isn't it?' she asked with burning, naïve hope. 'Do you believe in premonitions? You know, when I first saw him last year, I felt as if someone were clutching my heart, tightly and softly, both at the same time, I can't explain it, like when you're holding a bird in your hand and you don't want it to get away but you don't want to hurt it either . . . you know? Oh, I'm being ridiculous, but I swear to you I felt and understood that he was the one, he and he alone.' She said the words quietly: 'He . . . he . . .' Then she fell silent, covering her eyes with her hand.

'What if I'm wrong, in spite of everything, what if he doesn't come back, if he dies without having had me as his wife . . . Oh, I would have liked to . . . just once, just once . . . At least I'd have that.'

'No, don't say that. You don't know what you're saying. You mustn't speak of such things, you have no idea what you've lost.'

Colette stood up, went over to the window and looked out at the empty street.

'Have you spoken to your parents?' asked Rose.

'No,' replied Colette without turning round.

'Why not?'

'I daren't. Not now. Oh, they won't be unhappy. But . . . already Mama suspects and seems to be asking, "What can she see in him?" I don't want to talk to her about it yet. With you, it's different. You understand.'

'Yes,' said Rose wearily. She stood up, put on her coat. 'Come on. Let's go out. It smells of mothballs in here. It's dark and depressing. Come on.'

They left and wandered about aimlessly. It was hot outside. They were carrying their gas masks and felt ridiculous. Rose automatically studied all the women who passed and thought, 'She has someone out there. But that one doesn't.'

It was in their eyes, on their faces, in their vaguely absent expression; they looked as if only their female bodies remained while their souls were far away, following a train full of men, or a truck as it travelled down a road. Two young girls ran by, laughing. Behind them were an elderly couple.

'Suzanne! Charlotte!' their mother called out. 'Behave yourselves now. Don't be so insensitive.'

'But *we* don't have anyone going. Don't make us stop laughing.'

Rose went white and stopped.

'Let's go home,' she said quietly. 'It's too hot. I don't feel well.'

All the Parisians were saying they would be bombed that very night. They waited, without real fear, but with curious fascination, as a bird waits for a snake to appear. You can't run away, but the danger seems too unbelievable. You can't understand it; you can't imagine it. 'Whatever happens, happens,' everyone said.

That night, for the first time, they heard the sirens, that sound of rushing air that seems to rise up from the horizon, hurry towards you, growl like a storm, then moan, cry, whimper: 'All I can do is warn you. Escape! Death approaches. You are helpless. Run!' That night, almost everyone went down into the cellars. It was the first time. People laughed, showed off, felt pride in their hearts to be soldiers like the others. Ah, no one could say that the country was divided in two any more, as it was in 1914, with some who died and the others who profited from their deaths: everyone was equal, everyone was fighting, they were all risking their lives.

Pierre did not want to take shelter; he was afraid the basement would be too cold for his old wound. It was more painful in the damp. Agnès wouldn't leave him. Colette and Rose wanted to stay, but Agnès forced them to go. The inner courtyard was filled with the little lights of pocket torches. Never had anyone seen so many stars in Paris; without the glare of electric lights they flickered gently, making the sky look friendly and peaceful.

Pierre and Agnès pretended to sleep; his arm round his wife's shoulders, Pierre forced himself to breathe regularly, but she wasn't fooled. She knew he couldn't sleep.

'You're still awake,' she whispered in his ear. 'What are you thinking about?'

'Guy.'

He had answered at once, his voice weak and broken. 'How he's aged,' she thought.

She moved closer to him, pressing him against her, rocking him as if he were a child. To her, he was forever young. In her mind, her son who was gone and this soldier from the last war became vaguely confused. But as she held him close in the darkness and felt the scar on his hip, she remembered that he was fifty-five, that he was old and frail. An indescribable feeling of sadness, a combination of pity, fear and love, merged with all the other sorrow of the past few weeks. She pressed her mouth to Pierre's ear. 'My poor dear, my poor darling . . .'

'Ah, Guy,' he said again, gently pushing her away, as if the very touch of his wife was unbearable to him. 'Our little boy . . .' He sighed.

'He knows,' thought Agnès, 'he knows exactly what our child is facing. I shudder, wonder, imagine, but he . . . War, victory, battle, they aren't just words to him as they are to me. *He* knows what they are. He remembers. He knows where his son is being sent.'

'No one should have to live through that twice,' she said.

But he wasn't listening. He was speaking quickly, his voice full of passion. Far away in the distance they could hear the sound of gunfire; the anti-aircraft artillery was shooting at the enemy planes or carrying out exercises during the night air raids, to teach the Parisians to be cautious and patient.

'Did you see how they left?' he asked.

'Yes.'

'And what did you think?'

'I think it was nothing like in 1914 when the soldiers left. No flowers, no fanfares, but . . .'

'Yes, of course,' he cut in, 'they're marvellous. They're our lads; that says it all. If they have good commanders, if everything goes according to plan, they'll make it through, as we did. But . . . I'm afraid. Too many people have told them about the last war. The ones who fought in it remember it only too well. Collective memory is a terrible thing. They say that people tend to forget; yes, they do, but the way animals forget: they remember having suffered, but not why . . . This kind of memory is instinctive, full of blind resentment, injustice, hatred and stupidity. In 1914 we were as innocent as newborn babes. We went off cocksure. But they . . . they know that all our sacrifices were useless, that victory conquered no one; they've read, or seen, or heard everything that happened then, and since then – how do you think they're supposed to bear it? The young have heard our stories from the cradle. How often have we told them how stupid it all was, how pointless. And now? What will happen? Some of them, the good ones, the really good ones, won't even have the illusions they need to die a more or less decent death. As for the others . . . the majority . . . if the war lasts, there mustn't be any brilliant victories at first, otherwise they'll feel duped, like we did. But for us it happened towards the end. We held on, put up a fight. We carried on out of habit. But they . . . And to think we believed we had atoned for them, as if you could atone for an entire generation, an entire race, unless you're God . . . I'm very sad, very worried, Agnès; you're stronger than me, my darling.'

'Come on now, you're tired . . . in pain,' she reassured him, gently rocking him. 'Your hands are so warm. It's hot in here. As soon as the air raid is over we'll open the windows. Stay here. Don't move. Try to sleep.'

The night passed. In the first light of a joyously beautiful and rosy dawn, as pigeons cooed on the rooftops, the sirens announced the end of the air raid.

# 26

Along the dark, freezing streets of Paris, people lit their way with small lanterns that cast a cold bluish light into the black night, blinding the other passers-by. Snow was falling. Men and women stopped for a moment in front of a newspaper stand. They blew into their hands, unfolded the paper; beneath the electric light they looked for the official statement on the first page: 'Nothing new to report from the front.' They continued on their way down the slippery street. Paris had been lucky, so far, but in the silent shadows it seemed to be expecting something terrible to happen. 'How sad Paris is,' thought Guy.

He was home on leave, having spent the beginning of winter with the troops advancing towards the Maginot Line, and the days were slipping past, trickling through his fingers like drops of water; he could not stop time. The first hours had been wonderful, full of a physical sense of warmth and contentment. The bath, the bed, the clothing, everything felt so soft, so good against his body. He experienced the exhilaration of a traveller who finally stops at an inn and sits down at a table next to the fire after a long journey through the night, through the mud.

But as his departure grew nearer, his sense of well-being dissipated, gave way to a strange feeling of anxiety. In Paris he was spared nothing. 'What a strange war,' the civilians said. They congratulated him on how well he looked. 'So it's not so bad, this existence?' People were surprised that they hadn't yet marched into Berlin, weapons on shoulders. Even his father, his own father, who must still remember, had seemed a little ... naïve ... Yes, he couldn't find any other way to express it: naïve in his judgements, in his questions.

Rose wasn't as he remembered her any more either. She had lost her prettiness, and her face was fuller and paler than before. Only at night did he find her again.

That evening, two nights before he was to leave Paris, they decided to go out to dinner alone, just the two of them, without the family. She wanted to go to a little cabaret on the Ile Saint-Louis where they had secretly gone several times together when they were engaged. There was too much snow to take the car; they made do with the Métro. They walked towards the Ile Saint-Louis, arm in arm, in silence.

Suddenly Rose asked, 'What was the name of that woman ... you know?'

'What woman?'

'The one you wanted to ...'

She stopped walking for a moment, let go of Guy's arm, leaned against one of the parapets along the Seine.

'The one you wanted to kill yourself for,' she continued, her voice muted and as if terrified of herself.

'Why are you asking me that?'

'What was her name? Just tell me her first name.'

'Nadine. Why are you asking me this today?'

'No reason,' she replied. She took his hand again and leaned gently against him as they walked. He could feel his heart pounding.

'Was she a blonde? A brunette?'

'Blonde.'

'She was very beautiful, wasn't she?'

'I don't know.'

'What do you mean?' she exclaimed, annoyed.

'I swear to you,' he said, 'I don't know. All I remember, the only thing vivid in my mind – I don't know how to explain it to you – is what I thought, what I felt, how I suffered . . . Man is an egotistical animal. And as for her, her face, her body,' he said more quietly, 'all that has faded away. But please, let's not talk about it any more. It's painful for me.'

'Just one more question: did you ever see her again?'

'No.'

'Word of honour?'

'Word of honour. But what's going on, Rose? What's the matter?'

She gently rubbed her forehead against Guy's shoulder. It was not so much a caress as the kind of gesture you make to put pressure on an injured part of your body; it hurts more but makes it feel better too.

'It's since you left. Before, I was at peace. You were truly mine. I had . . . made you feel settled, do you understand? But out there, alone . . . men get bored, they think about things they wouldn't normally think about in everyday life. She might have written to you.'

'No, my darling . . . You're being silly.'

'You might dream about her.'

'Listen, Rose, I can't even remember the colour of her eyes. Nor the sound of her voice. It's forgotten, over, dead,' he said. But he was thinking, 'That's half truth and half lie, but . . . it's what I have to tell her.'

She took a deep breath with a little whistling sound, like when you come up from under water. 'Forgive me. We'll never speak of it again. I'm so happy, if you only knew, I feel free again and now I can tell you . . .'

'Tell me what?'

'No. In a bit.'

'But what is it, come on, tell me.'

'In a minute,' she said again. 'In a minute,' and she led him towards the door of the restaurant.

They went inside. The little room was brightly lit, full of people. Some friends waved to them. They chose a small table at the side.

Rose took off her gloves. 'My hands are frozen. But it's so nice in here, so warm. Look how busy it is. It's the same everywhere. In restaurants, in the theatres, it's always crowded. You wouldn't think there's a war going on.'

'Are you going to tell me now?'

'Tell you what?' she said, smiling.

They stopped talking; the waiter wanted to take their order. They chose their meal and the wine with great care. Now and again they were able to forget the war, forget his imminent departure, or rather, they didn't forget, they just hid it away deep in their hearts. 'Oh, too bad,' they thought, 'who knows what tomorrow will bring?'

He poured her a glass of Chambertin.

'Let's drink to the health of our child,' she said, 'to the child I'm going to have.'

'Rose? Is it really true?'

She nodded; yes, it was true. She had known for a few days.

'I saw Dr Lange, you see. But I didn't want to tell you right away. I didn't know what to do. I'm not sure why; you seemed so distant. It's horrible, this war . . . No, don't laugh. I'm a woman, and childish. But what can I do? I see things like a woman. You were snatched away from me, from my arms, from my bed, and thrown into a man's world, a harsh world that I detest. Do you remember that book you made me read, the one you like so much, where a pilot, a commander, a leader of men laughs because the wife of someone he's sent to his death is waiting for him to come home, with a lamp lit on the table and flowers on the tablecloth and clean sheets on the bed? But she was the one who was right, and I, I . . .'

He wasn't listening. 'When is it due?'

She counted on her fingers. 'End of May, beginning of June. A nice month to give birth, don't you think? I always thought I'd like to have a baby at the start of summer. The bedroom full of flowers, so cheerful,' she said, her voice emotional. 'They give leave, don't they, for the birth of a child?'

'I'm very happy,' he said over and over again, without looking at her, feeling oddly shy. 'Very, very happy.'

It was more than a feeling of happiness; it was a sensation of triumph. Everything around them was so full of danger: the night, the harsh winter, the war. And then, suddenly, this hope, this child, this joyous defiance of fate. 'Ah, you can mock me, but I can mock you as well.' He felt as if he were staring at his destiny and speaking to it, without hatred, but thumbing his nose at it, just as an arrogant schoolboy might say to his teacher, 'You want to destroy me but I'm still alive. You want to take away all my hope? But look: I'm married, I'm in love, I'm enjoying life, I'm having a child. And the more you try to beat me down, the more I'll fight you.'

He half closed his eyes and raised his glass to his lips. 'I'm so happy,' he said. 'Thank you, Rose.'

# 27

At the beginning of May, Monsieur Hardelot-Demestre arrived in Paris. He carried a small suitcase and his gas mask was slung over his shoulder. No one walked through Paris with this tin cylinder any more, despite the regulations, and Monsieur Hardelot-Demestre caught people looking at him rather mockingly. He walked briskly, his little white beard fluttering in the gentle wind. It was a warm, lovely day and the sky was very bright. You could sense a carefree, joyful laziness wafting over Paris; everyone was happy to see the end of the long winter and its cold darkness. The war continued, but there was so little fighting, so far away. Café terraces were full of people. Profitable deals for supplies were spreading by word of mouth. People were thinking about the changes in the Cabinet and betting on who would win. Monsieur Hardelot-Demestre found Paris charming. He had been a student there fifty years before; it was he who recommended the Hôtel des Grands-Hommes in the Latin Quarter to Pierre's parents; its gloomy little rooms had housed two generations of Hardelots.

During the war in 1914 he had visited Paris twice, once to see his only son who had been wounded and was being treated in a Parisian hospital, the other for the 14 July victory celebrations, when the Allied troops had paraded beneath the Arc de Triomphe.

Unfortunately he had set out too late; he'd been pushed back against the window of a little cheese shop, which he'd stared at for four hours before going home hungry and with his new umbrella broken, but still cheerful. Now, he looked at the capital with an indulgent, rakish smile, as if he had just pinched a young girl's bottom. He was a lively, mischievous old man. His wife had never been able to keep pretty servants for long. Monsieur Hardelot-Demestre imagined how he would convince his nephew, Pierre Hardelot, to take him out to the Paris Casino, and just thinking about it lit up his normally thin, pale cheeks, as well as his heart. Pierre Hardelot didn't know he was coming. He was there on serious business; if it was going to be successful, the old man thought, Pierre had to be taken by surprise. So he arrived at the Hardelots' home just as they were sitting down to lunch, Pierre between Agnès and Rose. Everyone was surprised to see him; they asked if he'd like to eat with them. He accepted a piece of the omelette with pleasure; he ate slowly, enjoying the curiosity of his relations.

After a while, they asked him if he would be staying long in Paris.

'No, no,' he said. 'I expect to be leaving in two days.'

He stopped for a moment then continued, 'With at least two of you.'

Agnès and Pierre looked at each other. Rose put down her glass without having taken a sip. Her pregnancy was very obvious and even her face was heavy and swollen. Every now and then she placed her hand on her bulge in a gesture common to pregnant women, as if she wanted to protect her child from some invisible danger. All three of them guessed the truth. Madame Florent's letters, fuelled with gossip from Saint-Elme, had suggested that Simone might be preparing to make peace, or at least to accept a truce.

'I come as an ambassador,' Hardelot-Demestre explained. 'I have been sent by the people of the Rue Blanche.' (In Saint-Elme,

people were never called by their names; they were described by
allusions: 'The ones from the Place du Marché; our friends who
live near the bridge . . . beside the château . . .' The Rue Blanche
was where the Renaudins used to live, before Simone had become
Madame Burgères. She had moved away, but she and that street
would be as one until the last of the Renaudins had disappeared
from this earth.)

'There's news,' he continued, gently stroking the end of his
beard, 'good news and bad news, as they say. Some that will hurt
you, my dear Rose, and some that can only please you, as long
as you are both prepared, you and Guy, to forget about certain
misunderstandings between you and your mother.'

'Is she . . . worse?' asked Rose quietly.

'Alas, yes, and that is the upsetting part of my message. When
the war started she took on an enormous amount of work, as you
know. Her male colleagues were mobilised and she never trusted
women. To sum it up, she worked too hard and had quite a serious
heart attack; and her physical condition influenced her morale.'

Rose cut in. 'She isn't in any danger?'

'No, she isn't . . . But what can you do? She feels old; she's all
alone. Her existence is gloomy. She loved you more than you
knew, my dear child. She has a tyrannical nature, so maybe she's
unhappy because she has no one to tyrannise,' he said with a little
laugh. 'Forgive me, Rose, you know that I have the utmost respect
for Madame Burgères. In any case, she wants to make up with
you. Once the war is over, she would like to share the burden of
power with Guy and, until then, she is asking that you, Pierre,
come to her at once. Her very words were, "Ask him to come
quickly, to hurry," to help her run the factory, for she is at the
end of her tether.'

He insisted for a long time before Pierre agreed. Perhaps Pierre
did not want to admit the inner satisfaction he felt; his inactivity
weighed heavily on him; he felt weak, useless, old. Energy flowed

through his body at the idea that he would work again, have problems to resolve, orders to give, responsibility. At times the factory had seemed horrible to him; now he thought about it nostalgically, as a widow thinks of a husband who may have been cantankerous but with whom she shared her bed for nearly twenty years.

He resisted for a long time, however, out of a sense of decency. They ended up by assenting. Rose, it was universally decided, must immediately defer to her mother's wishes. It would be better, more fitting, if the child were born in Saint-Elme, where from now on he belonged, to a certain extent. So Rose would leave the next day. Pierre would accompany her and, once there, he would see; he would speak to Simone; he would decide one way or the other. As for Agnès, she would go along as well and take advantage of the trip to spend time with her mother.

They planned the future slowly, cautiously, choosing their words carefully, prudently, like a child building a house of cards while holding his breath. However, the child understands that the house is fragile, while these middle-class people were certain they knew what tomorrow would bring. Despite Europe's terrifying chaos, despite the social problems, despite the wars, they had inherited a sense of security; it was passed down through their blood. They counted on the future just as their forefathers had before them. The months, the years to come unrolled before their eyes in slow waves, in gentle undulations, like the flat fields and roadways of their home. Even the smallest detail was planned in advance: Rose decided she would give birth in her mother's house; in her mind she was organising the large linen cupboard where she would keep the baby's clothes and picturing, in the alcove, between the prayer stool and her bed, the baby's cradle. Agnès was already worried about moving in October, if Pierre decided to stay in Saint-Elme . . . unless the war ended between now and then. She sighed. How sad. The war wouldn't be over. It would last as long as the one in 1914. Many people thought the same.

The events of the past cast a long shadow and their bloodstained light coloured the times they were living through. They could imagine nothing but the repeat of those four years of glory and horror, the immense, superhuman need for patience until it might end. Pierre dreamed of his son's return. He himself had come home safely from the last war and that seemed a pledge of good-will on the part of fate towards the Hardelot family. Once Guy was home, Pierre would say to him, 'Everything is in order. I've worked hard. I've kept your house safe for you.'

And so, as his grandfather had believed with such unshakeable faith, it was decreed that the factory would remain in the hands of the Hardelots for all eternity. Only the elderly Hardelot-Demestre was thinking of more immediate, more easily achievable rewards: a trip to the Paris Casino that evening, and the following week a wonderful, if discreet, dinner to celebrate the reconciliation between Simone and her children. He drank his coffee, making little slurping noises, and planned the menu: a good thick soup, some lovely fried sole, roast beef, a juicy chicken, asparagus and an ice-cream bombe.

The radio was playing dance music interspersed with snatches of political speeches; it washed over them like warm milk; they were only half listening. They paid more attention when the news bulletins came on, but there was nothing to report. Rose went to lie down. Agnès went out to do the shopping. The two men remained alone, discussing factory business and talking about Saint-Elme.

That night, 10 May 1940, after spending the evening at the Paris Casino, Hardelot-Demestre went to sleep and dreamed about a little dancer with rosy skin, who wore a G-string covered in golden stars and leaned over him to pull at his beard using little tongs. In his dream, Hardelot-Demestre was tickling the dancer; she resisted, let out tiny birdlike cries, then grabbed a toy trumpet (the old man had played with such a trumpet when he was a child

175

and he had never forgotten the power it had, its strident sounds, the red and yellow tassels that decorated it). The dancer whispered something in Hardelot-Demestre's ear but, little by little, her whispering became increasingly mournful, loud and alarming until Hardelot-Demestre woke up, rubbed his eyes and realised he was hearing the sound of the air raid sirens. The Hardelots had made up a bed for him at their home. He hesitated. Instinct told him to go down into the basement and, besides, he respected the laws that required everyone to take shelter whenever there was an air raid because one of them might prove dangerous. On the other hand these Parisians might make fun of him. So he waited, then coughed a little, so Pierre and Agnès, whose room was next to his, would know he was awake. After a while he heard them get up and come and stand at his door.

'Did something wake you, Uncle?'

'I'll say. What's going on?'

He understood by the tone of their voices that they were smiling.

'If you can't sleep, slip on a cardigan and come and have a cup of coffee. The anti-aircraft defence system is making a racket.'

They all met up in the sitting room. Agnès lit the gas cooker in the kitchen and soon brought them some steaming hot coffee. All of Paris was awake; the weather was too lovely, too warm; people couldn't stay tucked in their beds while the birds were singing with a kind of joyful intoxication. Out on the terraces women walked slowly back and forth in their dressing gowns or pyjamas. On the balcony opposite the apartment where the Hardelots lived, a very pretty blonde with dishevelled hair looked up at the sky. Agnès too went over to the open window and gazed up.

Hardelot-Demestre followed her. He cleaned his pince-nez, stared at the birds as they flew from north to south. 'The planes must be coming from over there,' he said. 'We'll be able to see them soon.'

But the birds obeyed their own laws and paid no attention to the planes; or perhaps the planes were simply too high to worry about, up there in the dazzling blue. They were invisible. Only their sound told of their presence, like a cloud of hornets in a summer sky – and the furious sharp explosions that seemed so close by. Agnès had planted flowers on the balcony. It felt strange to see these sweet peas entwined in the railings, though no one could say why. Stranger still was to feel the first rays of sunshine on one's neck and cheeks, to breathe in this innocent May morning air while hearing the sound of gunfire. No one was terribly worried; it was a false alarm, like so many others, but it put their nerves on edge and made their senses more alert. The beauty of this spring dawn pierced their hearts and filled them with pain, as if a sharp needle were hidden beneath all this sweetness.

At last, Pierre motioned to them. 'Oh, that's it, it's over.'

He had heard the first blast of the all-clear, that sound which is like a deep breath pulling in all the surrounding air before releasing it in a wail that is both a bellow and a lamentation.

They drank the rest of their coffee and went back to bed.

At that very moment the enemy was marching into Belgium.

# 28

The Hardelots didn't delay their journey because of political events; quite the contrary, they hurried to get to Saint-Elme. All of France was in danger and some vague instinct made everyone want to endure these perilous times in the bosom of their family. Nothing really terrible could happen along the calm streets between the factory and the church, thought Rose. Of course, during the other war, Saint-Elme had been destroyed, but we consider everything that happens before we are born as mythical, with no true link to reality. In Rose's mind Saint-Elme was indestructible. The dull, solid provincial family comprised of all the Renaudins, the Hardelot-Demestres, the Hardelot-Arques seemed as enduring to Rose as the rocks and the earth. She had never known her family to suffer, to be impatient, anxious, or want for anything in the world. If Saint-Elme were bombed, the thick walls of their cellars would provide safe shelter; their vast cupboards contained sufficient provisions to withstand a siege, she was certain of it. So what if her contractions began in the middle of a night-time air raid? The doctor who had delivered her lived close by. Even if she died, five pairs of arms would stretch out to take in her child; the entire region was full of friends and relatives. She trusted in Saint-Elme just as she trusted in her mother: harsh, bad-tempered, difficult to live with, but, nevertheless, a refuge, a rock.

Pierre and Agnès, however, did not share these feelings. They weren't the ones who needed Saint-Elme; Saint-Elme needed them. They were thinking about the houses, the people, the factory; they remembered various faces: the distant cousin who had three sons, all soldiers, the other cousin whose husband had gone to fight in Belgium. The workers needed the Hardelots; they were infuriated by the war and wouldn't put up with its ordeals for long without reacting with hatred and revolt; yes, they needed them, thought Pierre. There were so few men left in Saint-Elme. Of course, everything had been anticipated: civil defence, evacuation, if necessary, though this was hardly something to worry about. In spite of everything, Pierre said to himself, 'No one knows this place like we do . . .' His anxious heart beat with affection.

They arrived. Everything was calm. Children were playing. The workers were coming out of the factory. The little girls from the orphanage were going to prayers. The sky was a pure, dazzling blue. It was the season when all the lilacs were in bloom, so every house was full of flowers. In the lower part of the village you could see, through the rough lace curtains, large bouquets on dining tables set for supper. The ironmonger's and butcher's wives had them on their counters and in their windows, and from the open doors of the church floated the smell of lilac, as sweet and fresh as a trickle of water flowing through the shadows.

Rose did not expect to find her mother so ill. Madame Burgères was not in bed: in Saint-Elme, unless you were at death's door, taking to your bed was considered peculiar and somewhat disgraceful. She was waiting for her visitors in the little downstairs reception room, corseted, dressed, breathing with difficulty, sitting up straight in her chair. When she saw her daughter her cheeks turned red. She placed her hand on her chest for a moment,

with that anxious gesture common to people with heart problems.
She immediately looked at Rose's face and figure. Then she smiled;
Rose guessed that her fit, robust looks pleased her mother. A
healthy pregnancy was cause for pride in the family, like a son's
university degree or an ancestor's fortune.

'You look well,' said Simone.

They kissed, then stood facing each other, hesitant and shy.

'Have you forgiven me, Mama?'

'Yes, yes,' said Simone, looking away. 'I'm very weak,' she
continued. 'It's time someone took over from me.'

The front doorbell rang. People had heard that the Hardelots
had arrived and were coming to get the latest news. 'What are
they saying in Paris?' they whispered in anxious, subdued voices.
Women with grey faces, wearing mourning dresses and leather
gloves, wrung their hands as, one after the other, with courteous
greetings and apologies, they entered the sitting room. Each one
of them asked the same question, 'What are they saying in Paris?'

'But everything is fine,' replied Rose, 'just fine,' as she automatically offered her cheeks for the weak kisses of the ladies of
Saint-Elme.

Pierre and Agnès were staying with the elderly Madame Florent.
In the middle of the night, both of them woke up, at the very
same moment. They could hear the nightingales in the Coudre
Woods and, every now and then, a low, muted sound.

'It's gunfire.'

Where was Guy? Had he been sent to Belgium? He hadn't
written for several days. Pierre imagined himself back once more
in the fields where he had fought, where now, without a doubt,
his son was on the march. The evening news had been ambiguous,
hardly reassuring . . .

'They'll take a hammering at the beginning. It's always like
that for us at the start,' Pierre said to himself. 'They trust to luck,
make no preparations and stupidly send men off to be killed. Then,

at the very last moment, somehow or other things come together and everything turns out all right. That's how it was in 1914.'

Yes, that's what had happened in 1914 and it was impossible, unimaginable, that this time would be any different. He tried to reassure himself, but he was still restless. He got out of bed quietly, went into the dark sitting room, switched on the radio, twiddling the dial anxiously in an attempt to find a French or foreign station that might be broadcasting the latest information, for if he only could hear some good news it might ease the anxiety that was growing within him. He couldn't understand a thing. The sounds were muddled; other stations played bits of dance music. Finally, he made out a distant voice. 'All day long our troops have been engaged in bitter combat. Everywhere, they have tenaciously fought off the enemy . . .'

Angrily he switched off the radio, went over to the window and looked out at a rose bush in full bloom lit up by the moonlight, but without actually seeing it. Such a night, such a beautiful night . . . it clenched at his heart, filling him with feelings of indignation and anguish.

'Any news?' his wife called out.

'No, nothing.'

He went back to bed. Neither he nor Agnès could sleep. Lying side by side, staring wide-eyed into the darkness, they listened to the sound of gunfire.

Suddenly, Agnès sat up. 'On the road, down there, on the road . . .' she said.

'What? What is it? I can't hear anything.'

Then almost immediately he heard the sound of cars driving through the streets, the first refugees. They were recognisable, somehow: perhaps by the way they sped along the empty streets, perhaps by the impatient hooting of their horns, perhaps by the ever-growing rumbling sound as after one car came another, then another. And when they heard this strange noise, all of Saint-Elme opened their doors, their windows, came out into the streets, stared and wondered.

'They're coming from Belgium,' said Pierre.

They had both got up, crossed the hall and gone into the sitting room. The road passed a few metres from their house. Yes, they had guessed correctly; it was the first refugees. Mattresses were tied to the roofs of the cars and luggage spilled over on to the running boards and bumpers.

The cars continued to come all night long, all through the next day. No one had any news of the fighting, but they could sense defeat. There was something in the air, something heavy with despair, that seeped into the most isolated houses, the most peaceful fields, into each and every home, into the very heart of France. No one could sleep any more. Everyone had lost their appetite. They trotted out the same boring words of comfort: 'As long as they stand firm, that's what's most important . . . It's not that we've heard anything new . . . After all, in 1914 *they* only managed to get to Compiègne . . .'

They had no idea what was happening to Guy. No one knew anything about the men out there. They had suddenly all vanished, like passengers on a burning ship who disappear into the smoke and flames, before the very eyes of the few survivors. Now, it was the people of northern France who were fleeing. Everyone questioned them anxiously; where had they come from? Every day the places they named were a bit closer; some neighbouring villages had been bombed. No orders had been received; they didn't know whether they should stay or go. Each area had to look out for itself, relying on the courage or cowardice of a handful of men and often there weren't any men. A nervous woman, or a hysterical old spinster could evacuate an entire village, causing waves of refugees to flee along the roads and spread panic. Panic: it grew from one place to the next. It pervaded all of France, just as the sea rushes on to the beach during spring storms.

One day bombs finally fell on Saint-Elme. Planes appeared in the sky; they dived low, narrowly missing the rooftops. Moments later the little railway station seemed to shoot into the air, as if sucked up by a gigantic gust of wind, before crashing back to the ground in flaming pieces.

A few days earlier Rose and her mother had left Saint-Elme. Experience had shown that taking shelter in the provinces was not as safe as they had thought. Their walls and roofs were not bombproof, and their very way of life was buckling and collapsing. You couldn't count on anyone; people who had been considered pillars of society, up until now, revealed themselves incompetent and cowardly. Both the mayor and the ministerial representative had fled. Moreover, in the terrible confusion that began to reign all orders were suspect; no one could say with certainty if they came from French leaders or the enemy. The policemen disappeared; later on they learned they had been tricked by a misleading telephone call. Only a small group of men and women remained in charge of Saint-Elme and, among them, Pierre and Agnès held pride of place. This happened in spite of themselves. They were the only ones who had remained calm; they alone knew how to talk to people quietly, pleasantly, how to encourage them. They alone still thought of others throughout those days of blood and battle when so many could think of nothing but themselves, their own survival. All day and night, now, refugees from the north and Belgium passed beneath Agnès's window. The ones from the north didn't have cars. They slung packs over their backs; they carried their children in their arms. Old women ran through the dust behind their terrified cows. Someone found an abandoned baby in a ditch, wearing nothing but a vest and wrapped up in a tablecloth. Agnès could no longer sleep or eat. And besides, there was hardly any food left; what hadn't been given away had been stolen by bands of marauders who followed the refugees and mixed with them. And so, while Agnès fed the elderly, changed the babies, dressed wounds, gangs of men were getting into the kitchens, breaking into the cupboards, grabbing everything they could get.

There was no news from Rose. They hoped she had made it safely to Languedoc, where relatives would look after her. They still had heard nothing from Guy; there wasn't a single family in Saint-Elme who wasn't waiting, in vain, day after day, like the Hardelots, for a message that never came. In spite of everything, they lived in hope. Out of a pitiable sense of modesty, everyone kept their fears, their secret thoughts to themselves. The women workers from the factory who spotted Agnès on the street never said anything except, 'It doesn't seem to be going that well, does it?' Their tense faces were full of invincible optimism: 'It will be all right, won't it? . . .'

One night, news of the defeat at Sedan blared from the radio; it travelled through the open windows, out into the garden and over to the crowd of refugees. One man let out a cry: 'It isn't possible! We've been sold down the river!'

For a moment, everyone was so astonished that they fell quiet and through the silence came the sobs of the man who had spoken, a worker who had been wounded in the other war. The guns thundered. Someone called out from the road, 'Help me! I can't walk any more . . . Give me something to drink . . . Help me!'

Agnès, her teeth clenched, went from one person to the next, from the house to the gate, bringing milk, eggs, a crust of bread. Yet the night was serene and superb. A thousand stars were shining. The garden was full of white roses.

It was at that moment that she was handed a crumpled letter by a woman from Arras who had come back to the area to look for her children. Agnès read,

'Mama is very ill. We stopped on the road near Gien. We can't go any further. We have no more petrol and the roads

are so crowded that it is impossible to imagine how we can
go on. I'm afraid. Please come, I'm begging you. Rose.'

The woman was about to leave in a little truck and there was
room for Agnès. Once in Arras, the trains would be running . . .
perhaps.

'But we must stay together!' cried Agnès.

She had lost all heart. She threw herself into her husband's
arms. To die together, to suffer together, was nothing. But she
couldn't bear the idea of being torn away from Pierre.

'If it were for my son. But for her . . .'

'She's his wife, Agnès.'

'Come with me,' she said. 'What can you do here? Let's both
go. How am I supposed to get there all alone? Why are you
so determined to stay here? You can see very well that it's all
over.'

'You'll get there. You have to.'

'But what about you, Pierre? What about you?'

'Me? I'll stay here of course,' he said quietly.

For a long time they held each other close, silently saying
goodbye. Then Agnès left. Pierre had a moment of weakness. All
in all, why risk his life? Why give up the only consolation possible
in these terrible times: to die with his wife of so many years? He
wasn't a soldier any more. Who had made him responsible for
looking after the workers, the farmers of Saint-Elme? And what
could he possibly do for them?

But he didn't have time to feel sorry for himself. Along the
road, interspersed with the refugees, came the first of the defeated
soldiers, those who had survived in Belgium. The Germans were
right behind them. They had broken through all the defences;
they were flooding into the very heart of the country. At the
canal, a regiment was re-forming and, in an hour perhaps, there
would be fighting in Saint-Elme. The soldiers said that it had

been the same in the north. Civilians had been caught up in the tank attacks.

'You can't imagine what it's like until you've seen it for yourself. You just can't . . .' exhausted voices murmured.

'But then, what should we do for ourselves, for the children?' asked the women.

The soldiers shrugged their shoulders; they didn't know and didn't care. They felt they were destined to die; why should everyone else be spared?

A crowd gathered around Pierre.

'We have to leave. Leave, while there's still time,' shouted the women.

But he knew it was impossible. He could picture the crush along the road. And, most importantly, he believed that if the civilians continued to flee the army would be finished.

Near to Saint-Elme were the Coudre Woods, where excavations (the vestiges of a quarry) had left natural shelters; part of the population could take refuge there. Pierre thought for a moment, then said, 'My friends, go home quickly, pack up some food, if you can, and blankets for the children, and go into the woods. There are no military targets near there; the trees are nearly in full leaf at the moment and will hide you. God willing, you will be able to avoid the fighting, for our troops will mostly be defending the canal and the railway lines.'

As soon as he began to speak, everyone fell silent; finally someone was in charge, someone they knew, who was from Saint-Elme, whose clear, weary, slightly dry voice was familiar to them all. The stars lit up the anxious faces that looked at Pierre; he felt someone's warm breath against his leg and his hand touched the smooth little head of a child who had snuggled against him, feeling a reassurance and strength the boy could no longer find anywhere else. Pierre stroked his hair.

'You must hurry,' he said, 'but some of the men will stay here with me. If the Germans march in, they mustn't find the place deserted. But they won't get through,' he added, even though, at that very moment, he knew deep down that all was lost.

Silently, they obeyed. He watched the women from the factory run towards their houses, come back carrying bundles of blankets, dragging their children along by the hand. One of them cried out, as she passed the gate, 'But it's just so hard.'

Out of habit, she blamed her tough life on her boss. She carried two children in her arms; their heads stuck out of a quilt she had thrown over them.

Pierre took them from her. 'They're too heavy for you. I'll carry them some of the way.'

He held the children and the quilt close, and ran on ahead. The woman hurried beside him. Behind them came other women, rushing along frantically. When they got close to Pierre, he greeted each one by name. 'Hello Madame Grout, hello Madame François, hello Madame Vandeeke' and his composed, friendly voice calmed the terrified flock.

'You don't think it will be too awful, do you?' some of the women dared ask.

'Of course not,' he replied. 'Just one difficult night to get through. No need to be afraid; I'm here,' he added, smiling to himself at the naïvety of his words, but knowing how much store was set by simple words and especially by the sound of a calm voice.

Halfway there he handed the children over to their mother and headed back to Saint-Elme. The night was now vibrating with the roar of planes. They were still very high in the sky, very far away. Suddenly he heard the sound of an explosion and realised they were bombing the roads. That's where Agnès must be. He imagined the tragic confusion of horses, people and cars.

'I mustn't think about it,' he murmured, 'I mustn't. If we have to die now . . . well, it's better this way than being old and sick. Besides,' he thought, 'we'll make it through.'

When he got back to Saint-Elme, bombs were falling around the wrecked railway station. You could clearly hear the din of fighting. Pierre was sure the battle would take place at the canal, as in 1914. That canal was the key to the region; there was no doubt that Saint-Elme would be caught in the artillery fire of the opposing sides.

'There won't be a building left standing,' he said to himself. 'Ha! We're starting to get used to it around here . . .'

He waved to an old factory worker sitting comfortably in front of his house on a little wooden bench, his legs stretched out, smoking, as if it were a sunny Sunday afternoon. 'It's heating up, Monsieur Pierre,' the man said, taking off his cap.

'Oh, yes. It's a difficult time we have to get through.'

'What about your missus? She in the woods?'

'No. She's gone to Arras. Guy's young wife is about to have the baby.'

'She'll have trouble getting there. Seems like people are getting killed on the roads.'

'Yes . . . I know.'

'Anyway, you've got to do what you've got to do, Monsieur Pierre.'

'Yes. Are you staying here, my friend?'

'I don't want to leave my house.'

'I'm going to take a look around the village, make sure all my workers have gone.'

Patiently, he visited each of the houses in the workers' neighbourhood. He pushed open the doors with his shoulder, went inside, saw the empty rooms, the sheets trailing on the floor, the wardrobe left open (he imagined they had hurried to take the savings hidden beneath the sheets on the shelves and had left everything else). In some houses the fire was still lit, the beds made, a discarded newspaper lying on a table. He nearly fell over in the dark; he'd stumbled into a pram, left behind in the middle of a path. He hadn't gone far when he found three children in the dark of the François's house. Their mother had run away, leaving them on the large bed, crying; in the back room of the shop her paralysed grandmother had also been left behind.

'What can I do with them?' he thought.

There were many trucks left, but not a single can of petrol. First the refugees, then the soldiers, had taken everything. He got a garden wheelbarrow and lifted the paralysed woman into it.

'Jesus, Blessed Virgin,' she groaned, then whispered, 'save us . . .'

He grabbed the children, the pillows and the blankets all together, put them in beside her and headed back to Coudre Woods. It was slow going; with such a heavy load, the wheelbarrow kept slipping on the pebbles.

'Thank goodness it isn't raining,' he thought.

Twice, bombs fell close by. He threw himself on top of the wheelbarrow, instinctively using his own body to protect the children and the sick woman. The little ones talked incessantly. He carried on walking. At the second explosion he tipped everyone into a ditch.

Blazing flames now rose up from Saint-Elme.

'The church is on fire,' he said.

Everyone in Saint-Elme was so proud of that poor church: after it was destroyed in 1914, a daring architect had rebuilt it, using stones of different colours. He thought of Guy, of Colette, of Agnès, his heart breaking with love. He righted the wheelbarrow, picked up the old woman and put her in it.

'Now then, you see, you weren't hurt. Come along; no, children, get in quickly.'

Finally, they reached Coudre Woods.

'Is there any room here?'

He could hear movement beneath the trees, in the undergrowth. Anxious faces appeared.

'Are our houses on fire?' they asked.

'Yes, the ones near the station and the church.'

'That's my house,' said a woman, crying.

'Look after these children and push the wheelbarrow further away,' he ordered. 'And don't pay my respects to Madame François. What she did was vile; saving herself and leaving her children behind.'

'She was blind drunk, of course.'

He left, reassured that the survivors would be all right. Indignation over Madame François would make this woman forget her own problems and give her strength. Once again, he headed back towards Saint-Elme. How long the road seemed; in the past he'd covered it in a few moments behind the wheel of his car. It was the same road that, in his youth, had taken him to his secret meetings with Agnès. If he had to die, better to die here than anywhere else. He knew, he loved, every stone of this road.

A wall of flame seemed to hover in front of Saint-Elme. He couldn't imagine how he would ever get through. He covered his face with his hands and started to run.

'Is anybody there?' he called out. 'Is anybody still there? Answer me!'

Only the roaring of the flames replied. Planks of wood fell all around him and shattered. The factory was on fire. Two men knocked into him; they were carrying buckets of water and trying to put out the flames. But their efforts were in vain. Saint-Elme was lost. He needed to find any survivors who might still be among the ruins. He wandered from one street to the next, unable to see, choking from the smoke; abandoned dogs who had been left chained up filled the air with the sound of their terrified leaps and their heartbreaking howls. One of them had broken his chain and ran past Pierre, his coat on fire. Pierre picked up a bundle from the stream. A child. How did he get there? He was still alive. Pierre held him under his jacket. He went past the house where he had spoken to the old factory worker, barely an hour before. The house was on fire. The man had fled. Pierre was running now, holding the child close. Every now and then columns of smoke and flame rose up in his path. He skirted round them; he got through, he didn't know how. He seemed endowed with amazing strength and agility. Finally he made it back to the road. He ran, crawled, fell, got back up, eyes fixed anxiously on the woods, feeling himself responsible for every human being he had hidden there, for every breath that rose in their poor bodies. The woods hadn't been touched. He dropped down and rolled on to the grass, at the feet of a group of women who were scanning the horizon.

'Monsieur Pierre!' they cried out.

He was a terrifying sight; his clothes were in ribbons, his hair and eyebrows singed. The swaddled baby fell from beneath his jacket.

'My baby!' cried a woman, laughing and sobbing hysterically, 'my Jeannot! I thought he was with his grandmother. Oh, thank you, Monsieur, thank you . . .'

They brought him some water, washed his hands and face. Then, sitting on the grass, they stared at the fire. The flames were so strong at times that they could see clearly what was being eaten away.

Then someone would let out a sigh, a cry in the darkness. 'That's where I live; that's my house that's burning. Is there nothing we can do, Monsieur Pierre?'

'No, nothing. But our lives have been spared. The rest we can rebuild. Saint-Elme has been destroyed and rebuilt so many times . . . so we'll do it once more. Don't cry, Madame Vandeeke, and give me something to drink, please,' he said and his clear, low, clipped voice hadn't changed, the women thought.

All that night and all the next day they watched Saint-Elme burn. They also saw the retreating soldiers pass by, the ones who had managed to survive and not get captured after the battle at the canal, lost once more, alas. They saw the first Germans march through the ruins.

They couldn't even begin to consider organising any defence; they had neither men nor weapons.

'We must go now,' said the women, 'we must take the side roads and try to get to Arras.'

'No,' said Pierre, 'it's pointless. It's the same everywhere. What we must do is go back to our homes. Salvage what we can and wait for better times.'

Slowly, they all went back to Saint-Elme.

# 29

The flood of refugees was moving south, towards the Loire. The cars drove day and night. Their registration plates indicated where they came from; that was how everyone knew which regions were in danger. At first, only people from the northern and eastern provinces fled. 'It's always the same people who suffer,' they said, shaking their heads, remembering the military campaign in 1914. Then the inhabitants of Reims and its surrounding areas were evacuated in an orderly fashion; it didn't seem as if they had suffered too much during the journey. Next, everyone in the region of Paris got out, followed by the people of Dijon, Belfort and Yonne. Finally came the remains of the troops: carts and tanks, some still camouflaged with branches and leaves, carried a jumble of exhausted soldiers, along with women and children they'd picked up on the way. Agnès had managed to get hold of some petrol between Arras and Saint-Quentin. She was driving; Simone looked as if she were dying. Rose helped her mother-in-law as best she could, despite the tiredness caused by her pregnancy and the pain she was starting to feel in her back and legs; she took the wheel when Agnès needed to rest, for it was unthinkable to stop. There was not a single room, a single bed, a single square inch of space left in any of the villages; they had to keep going at all costs. Miraculously, they avoided the bombing of Vierzon. Barely an hour after they had gone, bombs fell on to the airfield. After Vierzon they moved off the main highway and took the smaller roads through the fields. These were less crowded and safer, but they led nowhere. They were going round in circles, constantly finding themselves back where they'd started. It was driving them mad. They knocked at doors, in vain; they were all locked, the houses empty. Some had been forced open and pillaged by the refugees. They kept going.

It was night; they had found some fruit in a town and, further along, they managed to buy a bit of soup at the buffet of a train station. Rose hadn't said a single word since morning. She held her mother in her arms; every now and then she pushed back the locks of grey hair that fell over Simone's eyes.

They crossed a small town in the centre of France. Here the crowd was less desperate. They still hoped the enemy would be stopped by the Morvan mountains. In a little café Agnès got some fruit, beer and hot tea for Simone. While they were eating, Rose whispered in her mother-in-law's ear, 'Don't tell Mama, but I don't think I can go any further. Is there a hospital here? Or a doctor, or a midwife who could take me in? I think . . . I think it will be soon.'

'Don't be afraid,' said Agnès softly.

'I'm not afraid,' the young woman replied. 'It's just that I know I can't go on.'

'I'll have a look around the town,' said Agnès, after thinking for a moment. 'I'll find a bed.'

The people wounded in the bombing had just been brought to the hospital by truck. They were stretched out on the floor; there weren't enough beds. In the few hotels, people were sleeping on billiard tables, in bathrooms, in the corridors. It was a sweltering June day. Agnès walked from street to street, to save petrol. All the roads looked alike with their little low houses, their gardens full of roses. She crossed a bridge. On the parapet two little boys with fat, swarthy cheeks were staring attentively as the cars filed past. She stopped for a moment beside them, utterly exhausted.

'There's lots of cars, aren't there, Madame, lots and lots!' one of them said, looking delighted.

He probably hadn't budged from this spot on the parapet for three days, thought Agnès; at this very moment he was most likely the only happy person in France. She smiled at him. 'Is it fun watching?'

'Oh, yes, for sure,' said the lad.

He took an apple out of his pocket and bit into it; he couldn't be more content, Agnès thought.

'You wouldn't know, by any chance, of a hotel or a house that could take us in? I'm with two other ladies and one of them is very ill.'

'Are you refugees?'

'Yes.'

'Me too,' said the boy. 'My mother was evacuated with her factory and my dad's a soldier.'

'Well, then, you must know the area. Think hard. Is there anywhere we could spend the night?'

The second boy, who hadn't spoken until now, cut in. 'My aunt has a lot of people staying with her, but you might find a room there. She's got a big house,' he said proudly.

'Well, where does your aunt live?'

'Oh, you have to head out of town and then take the first left turn. It's a mill.'

'Good, thank you; I'll try that,' said Agnès.

She returned to the café, got Rose and Simone back into the car and followed the directions she'd been given. It was indeed a mill. Water flowed beneath the arch of an old bridge with a fresh, primitive sound.

'A room? Ah, Madame, that's impossible.' The miller's wife raised her arms towards heaven. 'We already have people staying here who arrived from Paris yesterday. I gave them my own room and I'm sleeping in the kitchen.'

'All we need is a little corner, a small spot for my daughter,' said Agnès, her voice pleading, opening the car door and pointing to Rose.

The woman made a gesture of pity. 'Come in, at least, and have a rest.'

They went into the main room. Several people were already there.

A young blonde woman, wearing make-up, stood up as they came in. 'Madame, take my spot,' she said, offering her chair to Rose, who fell on to the heavy cotton cushions with a deep groan, feeling pain and relief both at once. Rose closed her eyes. Then they found a spot for Simone. Agnès sat down next to her, placed her hand on the elderly woman's burning forehead.

'Rose,' Simone stammered. 'Is she in . . . labour?'

'I think it will be soon,' Agnès whispered, 'but the miller's wife told me there's a good doctor very close by. Don't give up hope, Simone. We're safe here, I think. If only we could find a room.'

She had spoken quite loudly, on purpose. The young woman who had given them her armchair came over to her. 'Excuse me. I couldn't help hearing what you said. It goes without saying that you can have my room. I'll spend the night here, in the chair. It doesn't matter in the least.' She took Rose by the hand. 'Come along. You can stretch out and rest right now. The room is big and bright, and there's a chaise longue for Madame,' she said, turning towards Simone. 'But I don't know where we can squeeze you in,' she said cheerfully to Agnès.

'Oh, that doesn't matter,' Agnès replied, an expression of gratitude on her face, 'it doesn't matter at all, I can assure you. I don't know how to thank you, Madame.'

They got Rose and Simone upstairs. The room had a bare wood floor and was clean. They made up the bed.

'I've sent my boy to fetch the doctor,' said the miller's wife.

Agnès told her name to the young woman who had given up her bed for Rose. She started in surprise. 'Hardelot?' she murmured.

'Do you know me?' asked Agnès.

'My name is Nadine Laurent.'

'I am very indebted to you,' said Agnès, looking at her gratefully.

The young woman said nothing. She walked away from Agnès. When she reached the end of the corridor she turned and looked at her. 'If you need anything, don't hesitate to call for me, all right?'

'Yes, yes, I will, thank you,' said Agnès.

She felt like hugging the strange young woman. They had found shelter, refuge, somewhere to rest their heads. As for the rest, it would all work itself out. Rose was strong. The baby would survive, Guy's baby. There would be this child, at least, even if the others . . .

For a moment, she weakened. She hid her face in her hands. 'Guy . . . Pierre . . .' she whispered.

But she had no time to cry. She had to look after Rose. She had to boil the water. She had to get the few medical supplies she was able to buy in Arras out of the car. She had to find some nappies in the village. That, at least, would be easy. All the women in the house were rushing to help; one of them came in, followed by a young nun with a sweet, fresh face beneath her large wimple.

'I've come to offer you my help, Madame. I can look after the young woman until the doctor comes . . .'

Darkness was falling. Every night that June was serene, beautiful, solemn. The heavens leaned gently down towards the devastated land, the cities in flames, the poor men who had no food, no shelter. It lavished its perfumed air and the brightness of its stars on them, in vain; no one looked up at them.

It was four o'clock in the morning when the child came into

the world. It was a beautiful boy and Rose did not have a difficult birth. The miller's wife brought a cradle down from the loft,
the same cradle she had used for her own two sons, both of them
now away at war. The little wicker basket was clean and simple.
Hurriedly they attached to it a large, somewhat frayed sky-blue
ribbon. Someone knocked at the door.

Agnès opened it and saw the young woman who had loaned
the room to Rose. 'The Germans will be here within the hour,'
she said. 'What are you going to do? The whole village is leaving.'

Agnès pointed to the cradle. The young woman leaned over it.
'Already? The water in the millrace must have drowned out the
sound of the cries; I didn't hear a thing. Is it a boy?'

'Oh, she didn't cry out much. She's very strong. Yes, it's a
boy.'

'So you'll be staying, of course?'

'Of course. What about you?'

'I . . . I don't have any petrol.'

'I can give you the two cans I have left. We're going to have
to stay here for at least ten days, anyway.'

'You're very kind,' murmured the young woman.

She leaned over to study the newborn baby, her face filled with
a strange, mysterious emotion.

'Do you have any children?' asked Agnès.

She shook her head. The joyful, fresh, pink dawn lit up their
weary faces. The young woman knelt beside the cradle, looked
away from Agnès and asked very quietly, 'How is Guy, Madame?'

Agnès started with surprise and, suddenly, she was struck by a
memory. Nadine, where had she heard that name before? But of
course, Guy kept saying it when he was delirious . . . My God,
how long ago all that seemed!

'Do you know my son?' she whispered.

'Yes . . . I . . .'

She fell silent.

'I haven't had any news,' said Agnès.

Outside, they could hear the heavy, unmistakable murmur that rises up from towns and roads as the enemy approaches. Shutters were closed on the windows, doors locked, horses harnessed, wheelbarrows filled. In the streets the children, barely awake, all excited and happy at the idea they were going on a journey, laughed as they looked up at the sky. The sun was shining and, beside the mill, the water flowed green and frothy.

Rose called out. The nun at her bedside arranged her pillows, gave her something to drink.

Nadine stood up. 'Can you really give me some petrol?'

'Of course.'

'But how could I accept?'

'Well, I accepted your room for my daughter-in-law.'

'Oh, don't mention it . . . it was nothing.'

Their voices were cold now, restrained. Everything around them, the large room in the dawn light, the bare floor that creaked beneath their feet, the sound of the water, their words, everything had the fluidity, the fragility of a dream. Agnès walked Guy's mistress to the little outbuilding where she had parked the car; she gave her the two cans of petrol, shook her hand, watched her disappear. She went back up to Rose. She stumbled slightly as she walked; she felt so weary that she lost her footing twice and had to hold on to the handrail so as not to fall. All the travellers had gone. The large reception room and the kitchen were empty. But the miller's wife, looking quite calm, was grinding some coffee near the fire. Agnès sat down, or rather, let herself fall into a small, low chair. She felt tired, calm, detached from the rest of the world. She had seen her task through to the end. She had torn herself away from Pierre to find this young woman, this Rose whom she did not like. She had helped her as best she could. She had helped bring Guy's child into the world. All she had to do now was to accept, hope, wait.

After a few moments the nun joined them, leaving the door open in the room where Rose was resting. The coffee smelled good; the miller's wife sliced some fresh bread. They had made it through the night.

# 30

The Armistice had been signed. German soldiers occupied the village; they were sleeping at the mill, and in the morning the miller's wife cooked pork chops and omelettes for them. Rose was out of bed; the child was doing well. The period of rest had done Simone good, though it was obvious that this improvement could not last for long: she looked near death. The telephone lines between the Occupied Zone and the rest of France were working again. They managed to get through to Simone's relations who lived in the Languedoc and, one day, a car came to collect the Renaudin and Hardelot ladies. It was possible to travel now: the Germans allowed vehicles on the roads again and were getting things back to normal after the terrible confusion of the mass exodus. Agnès packed her small suitcase, kissed the baby, said goodbye to Rose and Simone. She was going home. She wanted to get back to Pierre in Saint-Elme. The other women didn't need her any more.

'You'll never make it back,' Rose told her. She was sure that Saint-Elme had been destroyed and that Pierre must have left, if he was still alive. 'He will have gone, I'm sure of it,' she assured her mother-in-law. 'He'll be able to find you easily at our cousins' house. He won't have stayed in the north; they say it's in ruins. It would be madness.'

'He's stayed at home. I'm certain of it. He wouldn't have left Saint-Elme. He was the only one left who could look after everything.'

'But what if Saint-Elme has been destroyed ... He wouldn't have stayed to look after ruins.'

'He certainly would. In 1914, my father-in-law stayed.'

'That was different.'

'Guy would have stayed as well, my dear girl.'

'They won't allow you to go back there,' Rose said again.

'I'll manage somehow.'

And so they parted, one heading south and the other returning north, to the region where no one knew what was happening, which seemed cut off from the rest of the world. Agnès had been travelling since morning when she learned that a Demarcation Line had been established along the Loire and that it was forbidden to cross it. 'If I had gone with Rose, I would have never been able to get back to my husband,' she thought.

Not for a moment did she doubt he was still alive. She knew she would find him. She pushed on, confronted danger, acting with the confidence of a sleepwalker making his way along a rooftop. A ghost seemed to be whispering to her, 'Do this. Say that.'

They refused to give her the necessary passes. They refused to give her petrol. They turned her away. She tried again, spending hours waiting at the Kommandantur.

'I have to get back to my husband,' she said. 'You can understand that, surely, Messieurs, that I have to get back home?'

She got what she wanted. Until the next stage of her journey. When she had used up her very last drop of petrol she continued travelling in trucks or old cars she came across on the way. Then the trains starting running again. Finally she could rest on a seat in a compartment. But just before they reached Saint-Elme they came to the Exclusion Zone. For more than a month she remained a few kilometres from her house, not knowing if Pierre was dead or alive, with no news of Guy or Rose, for it was forbidden to send letters between the German Occupied Territory and the Free Zone.

France was a tableau of heart-rending despair. Everywhere there were ruins, everywhere anxiety, mourning, tears and a sort of bewilderment that weighed heavily on people's souls. They went through the motions of living, without truly believing they were alive. Agnès, like everyone else, looked calm to the rest of the world, put on an air of dignity and gentleness. It was a matter of propriety. They all had to hide their bitter regrets, their tears, their fears about the future.

And then, one day, the miracle she had been waiting for happened. On a list of prisoners of war she saw Guy's name. A little while later she finally obtained permission to go home to Saint-Elme.

She travelled in a German army truck with other refugees. Every time they stopped the women with her asked about the villages that had been destroyed. But she didn't want to hear. She wanted to keep hope alive in her heart, just as you protect the flickering flame on a candle by covering it with your hand. As long as hope remained alive within her she was invincible, she was sure of it. Nothing could harm her. She was oblivious to tiredness, to hunger. And her hope and prayers protected her husband and her son.

She saw the ruins of some houses, a crumbling bridge, surrounded by nothing but scorched, deserted land. It was Saint-Elme. Some men were working beside the road, using pickaxes to knock down the remaining sections of unstable walls. They were the workers from the factory. Agnès called them over. They walked slowly towards her. In horrible anguish, she tried to guess what had happened to Pierre by the looks on their faces.

'My husband?' she asked quietly, as they stood in front of her. 'Do you know where my husband is?'

'He's in the canteen, Madame Pierre. He's going to be very happy.'

'He's alive, then?' she said and the joy that flooded her heart was almost painful. She went pale, brought her hands to her lips, held her wedding band tightly to her mouth so she wouldn't cry out.

'He hasn't been hurt?' she asked finally, after a moment's silence.

'No, Madame. Oh, he was lucky.'

The canteen was a hurriedly constructed wooden shack that they used to feed the children. Pierre was there. She stopped on the doorstep, trembling so violently that she couldn't move.

He seemed to sense her presence. He walked towards her. 'Is it really you?'

'My God,' he said, 'at last, it's you.'

Everyone was watching them. Embarrassed, they gave each other a little kiss. No kiss, no embrace could express the joy in their hearts.

They spoke softly.

'Guy is a prisoner of war; did you know?'

'Yes, I knew. What about Rose?'

'She had a beautiful baby. A boy. What's happening here?'

'Here,' he said, 'you can see what it's like.'

'We'll rebuild. We'll get through. We'll survive.'

She hid her face in her hands.

'You're tired, my poor darling,' he said, looking at her tenderly.

But she no longer felt any pain, any weariness. She felt that she had reaped her harvest, gleaned all the wealth, all the love, the laughter and the tears that God owed her, and now it was over, that all she had left to do was eat the bread made from grain she had milled herself, drink the wine from grapes she had pressed. She had gathered in all the good things of this world, and all the bitterness, all the sweetness of the earth had born fruit. They would live out the rest of their days together.